Praise for Heather Blanton

"Heather Blanton infuses her stories with immense grace and dignity."

— —LINDA BRODAY, *NEW YORK TIMES* BESTSELLING AUTHOR

"Heather Blanton is blessed with a natural storytelling ability, an 'old soul' wisdom, and wide expansive heart."

— —MARK RICHARD, EXECUTIVE PRODUCER OF AMC'S *HELL ON WHEELS*

"Fans of Louis L'Amour and Francine Rivers will find Blanton's stories even more enthralling. With wit, a clear author's voice, and storytelling chops that rival the best—you'll have found your new favorite storyteller!"

— —CARRIE FANCETT PAGELS, AWARD-WINNING AUTHOR

"Masterful at gritty fiction that points to the ultimate Creator, Heather will become one of your favorite Christian fiction authors."

— —KARI TRUMBO, *USA TODAY* BESTSELLING AUTHOR

LOCKET FULL OF LOVE

Also by Heather Blanton

Grace Be a Lady

Hell-Bent on Blessings

A Scout for Skylar

ROMANCE IN THE ROCKIES SERIES

A Lady in Defiance

Hearts In Defiance

A Promise In Defiance

Daughter of Defiance

A Destiny in Defiance

Hope in Defiance

A Reckoning in Defiance

In Time For Christmas: A Novella

LOCKET FULL OF LOVE

HEATHER BLANTON

Locket Full of Love
Paperback Edition
Copyright © 2025 (As Revised) by Heather Blanton

CKN Christian Publishing
An Imprint of Wolfpack Publishing
1707 E. Diana Street
Tampa, FL 33610

www.cknchristianpublishing.com

This book is a work of fiction. References to historical events, real people, or real places are used fictitiously. Any similarity to real persons, living or dead, is purely coincidental and not intended by the author.

All brand names and product names used in this book are trademarks, registered trademarks, or trade names of their respective holders. Wolfpack Publishing is not associated with any product or vendor in this book.

Paperback ISBN 979-8-89567-860-2
Ebook ISBN 979-8-89567-859-6

This book is dedicated to the hard-working authors of the Sweet Americana Sweethearts blog, who provide the world with sweet/clean historical romances about North Americans between 1820 and 1929.

LOCKET FULL OF LOVE

Chapter One

RIMFIRE, TEXAS, 1867

Had he lost his mind?

"Hugh," Juliet yelled after her husband. Fighting his way through a throng of panicked Texans headed for the bay, he didn't seem to hear. "For God's sake, Hugh, where are you going?"

"I forgot something," he yelled over his shoulder. "Get on the boat."

No. I won't. "Not without you!" She lunged after him, pushing, dodging, ricocheting off the mass of bodies flowing over her. Yet, in moments, she was able to slip her hand inside her husband's.

"I told you to get on that boat." Anger reddened his cheeks, and the flush was visible in his scalp through his thinning, ginger hair.

"I'm not leaving without you, Hugh."

"The Comanche are on their way."

"Then we'd best hurry."

Her husband's sweaty brow wrinkled with anger and frustration, and he dragged a hand through his hair. "Fine. We don't have time to argue."

He pulled her, hard and fast, and they were all but running. His long legs carried them quickly, challenged her to keep up with him. What could be so important? "Hugh, what did you forget?"

He pinched his lip, wiping away the sweat glistening in his mustache. "Your—your locket. We can't leave without it."

"My locket?" she practically squealed.

"It's the first gift I ever gave you. I must have it. *You* must have it, I mean."

Juliet thought he sounded almost dismissive with his explanation. Regardless, if the locket was this important—she hiked her skirt higher. "Then let's run."

The further away they got from the dock, the thinner the crowd grew. Another block and Juliet was convinced Rimfire was a ghost town. Surely, they would all make it safely into the bay to wait out the Comanche. The Indians were on a rampage. Most likely, they would burn the town and then move on, but if she and Hugh went to the water, they and the others in town would be alive to tell the tale.

At least, if they hurried.

Another hundred feet and then they scurried like panicked mice up the front steps of their neat, white clapboard home. They stopped in the foyer.

"Where is your locket?"

"Upstairs on my vanity."

He shot up the stairs, vaulting over them two at a time. Juliet took the brief pause in their race against death to say goodbye to the modest little house. She and Hugh had only been married two years, and this was their first home. She'd been so happy here. They'd planned and dreamed here, about children, his mercantile growing, branching out into ranching—

She stopped the woolgathering. There would be time for

that later. Hugh thundered down the steps, the locket swinging in his fingers. "Here, put this on and let's go."

He dropped the necklace around her neck and pulled her toward the door—

A shadow fell across the entrance, obscured by the frosted glass. Before she could react, the door burst in and a dozen whooping, hollering Comanches flooded into the foyer. Hugh blocked a hatchet wielded by a dark-eyed, screaming brave intent on murder.

But there were too many. Juliet screamed. Hands grabbed her. Like surging, angry flood waters, the Comanches shoved her and Hugh down the hall and out into the backyard. She heard the thuds and grunts of blows. Hugh was swinging, delivering vicious punches, but the braves retaliated with clubs and hatchets. Blood streamed down his face.

"Hugh," she screamed, reaching for him. *No, God, please, no—*

Their eyes met for an instant. "Juliet, I'm sorr—"

A rifle shot cut off his words. Hugh crumpled to the ground and Juliet screamed again. *No, no, NOOO!* The warriors' laughter nearly drowned out her own cries.

She kicked and writhed, but the dusky hands held her fast. Dark faces, painted in bright, primitive designs, peered at her...ravenous...curious. Her dress ripped, the sound as shrill as a banshee, and cool air bit her shoulders.

The braves laughed again and tugged at her corset, snatching her around by it, nearly giving her whiplash. One Indian, taller, thicker, meaner-looking than the rest, grabbed the garment with both hands just above her breasts and snatched, apparently sure it would rip apart just as easily as her cotton dress, or at least fall open and expose her.

It didn't weaken in the slightest. Juliet's shock turned to fury and she screamed and clawed at the savages. "Get away from me!" She kicked, punched, bit. Her struggle only evoked more howls of laughter from the attackers. Her golden hair fell loose from its pins and this seemed to amuse them as well, as they grabbed at the strands, yanking on it.

She was terrified, yet insane with anger. This was Hugh's fault. And God's fault. She lashed out with her nails, trying to pull flesh from anywhere her hands might fall, but she wanted more. Her mind boiling with madness, she wanted to wrap her hands around Hugh's throat and scream at him. Why wasn't he here to protect her? She cursed him and God.

Utter terror, coupled with a soul-scarring disappointment, seized her mind, burying it under this avalanche of crazed thoughts. She reacted like an incensed animal, snarling and growling at everything, everyone around her.

The tugging and pawing went on and on until a warrior new to the group appeared on the back stoop, bellowing something in Comanche. His comrades sobered immediately and rushed to the door.

Juliet barely had an instant to register her freedom and realize that she was still on her feet. Before meaningful thoughts could take form, the last brave, the mean one, sneered and fired an arrow into her chest. White-hot, breath-stealing pain bloomed in her breast like liquid fire. Pain so intense it crushed her lungs, froze them. The warrior spared not even a bored glance back as he turned away and Juliet crumpled to the ground. A black mix of agony and grief swamping her, she gasped a prayer, one laced with the bitterness of hate, the last she would ever utter. "Why, God? Why didn't You save us...?"

———

Juliet's eyes fluttered open. She registered the moldy, amber tent ceiling overhead but had to slowly turn her head to the left and to the right to understand she was in a hospital. Cots filled with patients stretched away on both sides.

She took a deep breath, and a pain as intense as lightning

struck deep in her chest. She let out the breath slowly, trying to mitigate the agony. An involuntary tear snuck out of the corner of her eye, raced down her cheek.

Desperately confused, she fought for her memory of what had happened, what had brought her here. Delicately, as if she were touching a baby bird, she rested a hand on her chest and touched a mound of bandage.

The arrow...

And the story rushed back at her.

Hugh was dead. Killed by Comanches. Tears sprang to her eyes again, but from a much deeper, much crueler pain. *And I live? Why do I live?*

Another thought, colder and harder, no sense of destiny in it, invaded her thoughts. *The locket. Why had he gone back for that infernal locket? If not for that, he would be here. Stupid, stupid man.*

A sob escaped her. The action provoked such torture in her chest that she clamped her teeth together to hold back a scream. She couldn't believe the intensity of the pain. She couldn't believe Hugh was dead.

How could he not have understood the danger? How could a piece of jewelry be worth this? God, why did You let this happen?

She closed her eyes and let the tears come, realizing it took less effort and caused less agony if she didn't fight them.

"Uh, Mrs. Watts?" A man's voice inquired uncertainly. Juliet sniffed, opened her eyes. A handsome young soldier with blond hair, inviting blue eyes, and a curiously straight nose, gazed down at her, compassion evident in his shaky smile. His blue uniform bespoke his military service, but his perfect posture would have given it away nonetheless. "I hope you don't mind. I wanted to check on you."

Too overwhelmed to object, she motioned miserably for him to sit. He licked his lips and perched on the very edge of the cot, pulling off his kepi. "Isham Good and I found you. You were pretty...well," he shrugged. "In a bad way. I'm glad we happened along when we did. Our unit got to Rimfire in time to run 'em off before they did too much damage. A few buildings burned, but mostly everything is all right."

Juliet turned her face away from him. Her throat squeezed in on itself. "My husband isn't all right."

"No, ma'am, he isn't. I'm sorry about that." The young man sighed softly. "I bet he'd be awfully relieved to know you're all right. God had His hand on you, Mrs. Watts. I believe your corset saved your life."

God? The mention of Him brought her head around again. The hands grabbing and groping at her while her husband lay dead only a few feet away was jarringly vivid. She could feel the grasping, greedy hands, probing fingers. No one there to protect her, God merely standing by and watching. "What do you think God had to do with it, Mr....?" She paused. He had not introduced himself.

"Oh, I'm sorry. I'm Private Robert Hall." He dipped his chin. "Your corset, of all things, gave 'em some trouble, guessing by the looks of it. It's cut up some, got a few punctures in it from knives, but when we pulled the arrow out of your chest, it was pretty clear the ribbing deflected the tip, and the material slowed it down. That's what *I* call a miracle, Mrs. Watts."

Yes, she supposed it was. She was alive and Hugh was dead. *That's what I call a miracle, Mrs. Watts. Be dutifully grateful, Mrs. Watts. God allowed Hugh to die, Mrs. Watts, but it is all part of His Great Plan, Mrs. Watts. Aren't you blessed?*

She wasn't inclined to think so. She was just angry. Angry with the Comanche. Angry with God. But most especially with Hugh. She thought she knew him better than this. She thought he loved her more than...than to risk her life for a trinket? How could he have put something so trivial before her safety? And if God loved her, how could He have let this happen?

A sob broke from her and she whimpered with the physical pain it caused. Private Hall patted her hand and she did appre-

ciate his kindness. "Thank you. I'm sorry I'm not more properly grateful."

"Oh, no," he waved her concerns away. "I understand.
Here, I did bring you something." He reached inside his coat
and withdrew his hand, clasped around something. "I thought
you might like to know this wasn't lost."

His fingers unfurled and the locket glimmered in his hand.
If Juliet could have gasped, she would have. If she'd had the
strength to toss the piece of jewelry across the tent, she would
have. Instead, she measured her breathing and said, "He died
for that locket. We were all the way to the docks, we could
have gotten away, but he turned around to go get that ridiculous piece of *frippery*." Her chin quivered, a knot constricted in
her throat. "I don't want anything to do with it, Private Hall. It
cost me *everything*."

The soldier sucked his bottom lip, nodded in apparent
understanding or at least compassion, and slipped the locket
back into his jacket. "Well, I can understand that, Mrs. Watts.
How 'bout I hang on to it for you? Would that be all right? You
ever want it back, just tell the Army."

"Fine." She stopped short of saying *thank you*.

He tapped his pocket. "Before I go, Mrs. Watts, would you
mind if I prayed for you?"

If she hadn't known it would hurt so much, Juliet would
have spat in the man's face. Instead, she managed through
clenched teeth, "Yes, I would mind a great deal."

Chapter Two

Major Robert Hall knocked on the door labeled *Senator Desmond Wilson.*

"Come," a throaty, booming voice answered.

Robert tucked his leather satchel underneath his arm and entered his former commander's office. "Sir," he said, saluting.

"Robert." The senator rose to his feet. Wilson's sizable bulk filled the room as his smile at seeing a former underling erased years from his craggy, bearded face. He offered his hand and the two shook. "Son, it is good to see you. I heard about your promotion. Congratulations."

"Thank you, sir."

"No *sir* anymore. *Senator* will do. Please, have a seat."

"All right. Thank you—" He bit off the reflexive *sir* and settled in a straight-backed velvet-covered chair.

"Can I get you anything?" Senator Wilson motioned to a cart nearby holding a decanter and glasses. "I have a fine port there, or I can have my assistant bring you some coffee."

"No, but thank you…Senator." Robert marveled over being treated as an equal by his former commander. While Major—

Senator—Wilson had always been a good, fair officer who valued the support of his military staff, he had never called Robert by his first name until now.

"I think I'll have a snort." The senator stepped over to the cart and raised the decanter.

The tiny, delicate sherry glass in his beefy paws looked out of place. During the war, Wilson had carried a leather-covered flask and guzzled his liquor.

The senator returned to his seat and raised his glass. "You don't know what you're missing." He took a sip and smiled, apparently lost in the fine wine. Shortly, though, he returned to business. "So, I suppose you are wondering why I've brought you down here from Army Intelligence? Another case of those ludicrous die-hard rebels trying to rob a train somewhere, you're thinking?"

Some of the Johnny Rebs wouldn't say *uncle* and were robbing banks, supply posts, anything they could get their hands on. A few had been caught, and the Judge Advocate General's Corps had prosecuted the cases, with Senator Wilson pushing for harsher sentences. But somehow Robert felt that wasn't the reason for this meeting. "I'm guessing not this time."

The senator's face hardened and his sixty years settled more clearly in his weathered lines and wrinkles. "The William Maxwell case." The name seemed to transform him from an amicable, overfed bureaucrat in a skillfully tailored suit to a wary grizzly, alert and looking for a fight. "I understand you've been following it, unofficially."

"Yes, sir. You questioned me about our rescue of Maxwell's wife back in '67. I've been"—he chose his words carefully, lest he sound obsessed—"*interested* in the case ever since."

"That's right." The senator snapped his fingers. "You plucked the arrow from her breast. It's been so many years, I'd forgotten that detail. But that's how you got started in intelligence, isn't it?"

That was *why* Robert had transferred to the Bureau of Military Information—Mrs. Watts's disappearance after the raid and the ridiculous hope he would see her again had drawn him in. As the years had passed, the mystery of her whereabouts had only fueled his desire to know her end. The Army had lost track of her in the chaos of the Indian attacks, leaving too many questions unanswered, and her last words to him ringing in his ears.

His move into intelligence, precipitated by his hope that he may find her more easily if he had access to certain resources, had revealed a troubling discovery that added to the mystery: the Bureau had been looking for William Maxwell, *A.K.A. Hugh Watts*, Juliet's husband, before the attack at Rimfire.

Initially a Union soldier, Maxwell had traded loyalties—either because he had been recruited as a spy for the North and given an assignment, or had become, in the worst case, a Confederate sympathizer. To muddy the mystery even more, there was no complete intelligence file on Hugh/Maxwell. Parts of it seemed to be missing or had been redacted.

During the war, Maxwell had allegedly protected the life of a Southern spy, an action that had resulted in the death of several men, some under his command, and some Union soldiers. The mysterious spy—the valuable cargo for which these lives had been sacrificed—had disappeared into the shadowy chaos of a train explosion and a Southern defeat.

After two years of searching, a vague trail of information had led the Army to Rimfire—only days before the fateful Indian attack in 1867. Once Juliet's marriage to Hugh—*Maxwell*, he corrected—was discovered, an investigation into her was opened as well. After the raid, though, she had walked out of the hospital and disappeared. Robert had believed the official file on her had been closed.

"We found her, your Mrs. Watts," the senator announced grimly.

Robert's attention snapped back.

"She owns a saloon in St. Joseph, Missouri."

"St. Joseph?" The amount of hope that jolted his heart surprised him. He attributed it to the potential of finally solving a decade-old mystery. Surely, nothing more.

"Owns a saloon there. Has for the past six years." The senator leaned back, the leather and wood of his chair protesting. "You still convinced she didn't know about her husband's wartime activities?"

Robert shrugged. "When we were removing the arrow, she was barely conscious. She called out for *Hugh* repeatedly. Never William. Looking back on it, I would still be inclined to say she was unaware of his activities. They did meet *after* the war."

"Doesn't mean he didn't tell her everything." The senator drummed his fingers on his blotter, his expression growing thoughtful, his gaze drifting far away. "Or at least a few choice details."

"Sir, I mean, Senator, if you don't mind me asking, why is her file active? I thought it was closed. I thought my investigation was a hobby, so to speak. Nothing official."

"But the Bureau was aware of it. And the simple answer is justice, son. Her husband was a traitor. A wretched, yellow-bellied coward who sold secrets to the South. Cost lives, on both sides."

"I believe there is the potential he was a Northern spy, sir —Senator."

"You've seen Maxwell's file. Nothing confirms that. I believe he went over. Crossed sides. The question now is: did she know? If so, she is complicit. She hid a fugitive. And the victims of Maxwell's treachery deserve justice. Don't you agree?"

"Yes, sir." The words came without thought, and he wished he could take them back because he wasn't so certain. Ten years. How long did one hunt justice? Was there no limit? No grace? Or was he simply making excuses for the fact that he didn't want to see Mrs. Watts as an accomplice? All these years, she'd been a helpless victim in his mind. A damsel in distress. An innocent.

"Spies were never pardoned or given amnesty by the president." The senator set down his empty glass and sighed. "I want you to go to St. Joe and investigate. If you still think she knows nothing of her husband's activities, we'll close the file and let it be. Mrs. Juliet Watts can disappear again. But I need at least very strong circumstantial evidence."

———

Juliet wiped down the bar as her eyes again drifted to the dress form in the corner—the dress form wearing her *famous* corset. Pockmarked with fraying tears from unsuccessful stabbing attempts, a brown blood stain in front, and years of saloon grime, it seemed to beckon to her.

Her hand slowed. *Why can't I stop looking at it today?*

She kept it there to entertain the customers, earn their respect. Any woman who could survive that ordeal deserved the best-behaved customers in St. Joe, or so the men extolled.

Maybe.

But Juliet really kept the corset out in full view so she'd never forget what Hugh had done. No noble sacrifice for another's life, no selfless act of courage had taken him. He'd died for a trinket. And love—heavenly, earthly—it was just a grand lie.

The old anger welled up inside her but she shook her head. *Not today.*

She huffed and tamped it down, resuming her cleaning chores, though there really wasn't much to do out here. Sam, the night bartender, had been kind enough to sweep and tidy up things. Even washed the glasses. Must have been a slow night. She glanced at the Regulator clock on the back wall. Ten o'clock. Ticking loudly in the early morning silence, it warned her the hardcore drinkers would be banging on the front door any time now.

She hurried across the saloon and unlocked the entrance, then returned to the bar. Crouching down behind it, she faced the safe and twirled the dial left, right, left again, and opened it to retrieve the money drawer. She rose with it in her hands and squeaked in fright.

A man waited at the bar. He snatched his dirty, tan cowboy hat off, wispy ash-blond hair falling across his forehead. "Ma'am, I'm sorry, I didn't mean to startle you."

Juliet took a breath, then paused. Handsome as the day was long, the man's blue eyes stared right into her soul, but she noticed his nose almost immediately. Not too big for his face, but a little long and perfectly straight. "I know you." She hadn't meant to say that aloud, but the thought had leaped right past her lips.

The man brightened and set his hat aside. "Yes, ma'am, you do." He motioned to her corset. "I helped get you out of that contraption." He frowned. "That didn't sound proper. I mean—"

"I know what you mean," she said curtly. "You're..." She slipped the cash drawer into its box just below the bar. "You're..." She snapped her fingers. "That private. Private Hall."

His smile expanded as he swept the hair back. "You remember my name."

He seemed so honestly delighted that Juliet couldn't hang on to her anger, but neither did she bubble over with gaiety. "I tend to remember people who pull sharp objects from my chest." His smile faltered at her deadpan tone and she was a little sorry for it. He'd only done her a good turn. She shouldn't be so waspish. "It's early, but I assume you're here for a drink? It's on me. My finest whiskey. Least I can do."

"Well, uh," he rubbed his chin. "I wouldn't mind. Would you mind if I came back at a more respectable hour for it?"

"No, not at all. What are you doing here now if not for a breakfast beer?"

He flinched. "No, definitely not that. I have something for you. I'm on my way to gold fields in Colorado. Heard there was a lady in town who had a special corset on display. I gambled that it had to be you. So..." He reached into his pants pocket and pulled something out. He held his hand up between them, loosened his fingers. She gasped. That infernal locket dangled before her like a hypnotist's prop.

After a moment, when she didn't reach for it, Mr. Hall slowly lowered his hand, his expression crestfallen. "I thought after all these years, you might..."

Forgive him? She thought bitterly. *Want to see his face?* She couldn't remember what Hugh looked like anymore. The realization hit her hard. She hated a *ghost*. A man she could barely recall. But she had been so in love with him at one time. It seemed like a hundred years ago.

Licking the dry off her lips, she reached for the locket.

"I haven't opened it or even looked at it since that day, ma'am. I figured you should be the one."

Juliet didn't really hear him. Her heart started racing as she once again held the oval-shaped locket in her hand, after all these years. Holding her breath, she opened it. Hugh—with his big, bushy mustache, receding hairline, thin face, and wide eyes—stared back at her. A strange mix of melancholy and surprise blew across her heart, kicking up dust devils of memories.

She suddenly missed being that young girl who had dreamed of a life with her handsome, ambitious husband, an up-and-coming businessman in the town. Remembrances of their brief time in Rimfire leaped to mind. A harvest dance where he'd made her feel like the belle of the ball, stoically but politely refusing to let any other man dance with her. And she hadn't argued. The purchase of their first home, a neat, white clapboard house with a long front porch.

Talk of children, seeing Europe someday, plans to become solid, valued citizens in Rimfire had put wind in their sails. Such high plans. So many dreams and goals to chase.

She cleared her throat, surprised it had tightened up on her. "I should say thank you." She drifted a thumb across Hugh's face and his picture, dry and brittle, fell out on the bar. "Oh." She picked it back up, but paused when she looked at the empty space in the locket. She tilted it left to right in the light, then did it again.

"What is it?" Mr. Hall asked.

"It's almost like..." She ran her thumb over the space. "Yes, see." She turned it to him. "It's almost as if there is a faint imprint of a key or something, and you can feel..." Again, she ran her fingers over the smooth metal. "It feels as if there is something behind the backing."

"May I?" He put his hand out and she dropped the locket into his palm. He peered at the piece of jewelry closely, carefully, running his fingernail along the edge.

As he investigated the locket, Juliet's curiosity about the locket gave way to an involuntary appraisal of Mr. Hall. She remembered that her first thought of him ten years ago was that he had such an interesting nose...and he was handsome. His blond hair shimmered in waves and slight curls grazed his collar. His face had some color, a healthy tan with a touch of pink on his cheekbones. He was no farmer out in the sun all the time, but neither did he live indoors.

His hands were clean, his fingernails trimmed, but there was evidence of a few fights or an accident on his knuckles. If she had the time, Juliet might inquire where he was from and what he'd been doing these past years. She did not have the time, however.

He tapped at the backing, skimmed his thumb over it. "I agree. It definitely feels like there is something in there. I assume St. Joe has a jeweler?"

"Yes, and I'll be going to see him." She slowly retrieved the locket from him. Their eyes locked, but his did not show challenge or surprise. Blue as a fabled tropical sea, they were warm and made Juliet's breath come a little faster. "Thank you for bringing this back to me." She bounced it in her hand and let the curiosity flood back.

"My pleasure. You wouldn't, uh, you wouldn't mind if I tagged along to the jeweler? I realize that's rather forward, but you can't imagine how curious I am now."

Oh, no, she thought she could. She was eager to rush over to Wilhelm's jewelry shop so fast that one might think her petticoat was on fire. She couldn't leave the saloon, though. Not yet. "I, um, I guess that would be all right. I'm pretty curious, too. To say the least. I can't leave till noon. When my bartender comes in."

"Noon then?"

She weighed his request for another second, but gave in. What would the harm be anyway? "All right."

"I'll be back." He slapped the bar in goodbye, picked up his hat, and headed for the door. Juliet watched him go, wondering why this simple *yes* to his request felt like something rather...destined.

Chapter Three

Robert ate a leisurely brunch and wandered around the
bustling river town of St. Joe, but kept a close eye on the time.
Five minutes to noon, he tucked away his pocket watch and
slipped into the Lost Sally Saloon, wondering who Sally was.
Juliet, handing a customer a beer, held up one finger, signaling
for him to wait. He sat down at a table, tossed his hat aside,
and studied the crowd of gamblers, sailors, salesmen, and a
cowboy or two—but mostly, he studied her.

When she'd stood up from behind the bar and their eyes
had met, Robert had just about quit breathing. The last time
he'd seen Juliet, she'd been pale, frail, and surviving a pretty
impressive hole in her chest. Long, golden tresses, messy, a
little dull, had curled around her face, covered her pillow. Her
eyes had been a touch sunken, highlighted by gray smudges
beneath them. She had looked so done in. Still, he'd thought
her beautiful then.

Now, she was stunning.

Her color was high, like her cheeks. Her eyes, green as a
mountain lake, sparkled with vitality. She wore her hair down,
some of it pulled back and tied with a ribbon. The locks shimmered with the light and looked as soft as down. Her skin

seemed to glow against the pale blue of her dress. Ten years and she was more beautiful than he'd dared hope. It was as if he'd known all along she was this beautiful.

He swallowed and looked away. What if she was a traitor? He couldn't believe it, but what secret did the locket hide? If she had something to hide, surely she wouldn't let him go to the jeweler with her. *Please, Lord, let her be innocent. And not as bitter as on that day.*

Of course, he'd prayed such before and, so far, it looked to him she was still swimming in bitterness.

"Ready?" She dropped the locket in her reticule as he rose from the chair.

"Yes, ma'am."

———

High noon in St. Joe reminded Robert of myriad towns he'd hunted through these last years. Busy, folks jostling each other in the street and on the boardwalk, as if getting some place five minutes faster would make a difference to their fortunes. And the smells. Unwashed bodies, sweaty horses, manure baking in the sun was common. St. Joe had one extra odor. Mud. He could smell the mud from the banks of the Missouri, a few blocks over.

He and Juliet ambled down the street together, but an awkward silence—not disguised by the whinny of horses and rumble of wagons—made conversation an effort. He was here. She was more beautiful than he'd dared hope. And he was at a loss for words. After all this time, he couldn't think of small talk? Robert clasped his hands behind his back and prayed for something to say. "So...how long have you been in St. Joe?"

"I bought the Sally four years ago."

"Did you stay in Texas for a while after..." He trailed off, wondering if her husband's death was too sensitive a subject to broach.

"No. I left almost immediately. I have family in New York. We came over from Ireland together when I was but a mere babe."

That explains a lot. "I didn't know you were from Ireland." And neither did the Bureau.

"Oh, shore and begorin'," she said, slathering her accent with her native brogue. "I was born in County Kilkenny. We left when I was barely able to reach the corner of me lovely mum's apron."

They laughed at her affectations and Robert breathed a little easier. Juliet seemed to be warming up a bit. "You don't strike me as the type of woman who likes a big city."

"Oh, I hated it," she said, rolling her eyes. "But I worked for a bit in a pub, saved my money, made my way here, saved up a little more, and finally bought the Sally."

He scratched his temple and turned to her, pulling his shoulder in to avoid a passer-by. "Why is it called the Lost Sally?"

"The way I understand it, a man named Salazar came to St. Joe in 1840 and opened up a trading post in the building. He went out one day to meet a trapper and discuss the price of some furs. He never came back. The building was sold in a public auction, and the next owner opened the saloon. He called it the Lost Sally, Salazar's nickname."

"Ah." Robert nodded, but then the conversation sagged again.

Mercifully, Juliet picked it up. "What about you? Where have you been for ten years? The Army didn't suit?"

Robert felt an undeniable twang of guilt. His answer would have to be a lie. He'd had to lie before, of course, in the execution of his duty, but lying to Juliet felt decidedly wrong. Still... "Mostly, I was involved in...aspects of law enforcement. Different venues." A puzzled *v* in her brow told him she was going to question that, and he decided to deflect. "Might I ask you another question about the locket?"

The *v* deepened, expressing her displeasure. "I suppose."

"When I tried to give you the locket the first time, and even today, you didn't want it. Have you spent all these years holding a grudge against your husband?"

She took a deep breath and slowed her pace, as if the question had hit too close to a painful truth.

Robert ducked his chin. "I'm sorry. That was too personal."

She laced her fingers over her stomach and nodded. "Yes. It was." She hunched her shoulders, as if fighting off a chill, though the day was warm. "I'm sorry. I can be a bit...surly. I want you to know, I've always regretted how rude I was to you that day. My apologies."

He shrugged. "You were under duress, to say the least."

"What did you do before the Army?" she asked abruptly, he assumed to change the subject.

"I was a cadet at West Point. A month away from graduation when war broke out."

"And you went home to...?"

"Massachusetts. Home of John Adams and goober peas." She chuckled and he breathed a little easier, glad some of the tension was slipping away again.

"Did you always want to go into the Army?"

"The only thing I knew when I went to West Point was that I did not want to follow in my father's footsteps." She pondered the answer with a troubled dip in her brow and Robert sighed. "My father is a mortician. A successful mortician, but a mortician."

She started to laugh and slapped a hand to her lips. "My, that's a...that's quite the profession."

He grunted. "You see my dilemma." He lifted a shoulder. "Not the job for me, though, I will say. At an early age, I learned the priceless value of life. One minute you're breathing and the next you're facing your eternal destiny." He bit his bottom lip, seeking a way to ask a question that had burned in his heart for years. "Will you bite my head off again if I mention God or prayer?"

Her face stiffened. She paused and turned to him. "We're here." She motioned to a door beside him.

Obliging, he opened it for her, but didn't think he kept the disappointment from his expression.

———

Holding the door, Robert cautioned himself to be a little gentler with Juliet. She walked past him into the jewelry store and he caught a whiff of vanilla, beer, and something uniquely her. It made him long desperately for something he couldn't even put into words. Praying for clarity and patience, he vowed to go easier. Push too hard and she'd push back. Push him right out the door. And he still wanted that whiskey with her.

"Mr. Mueller?" Juliet called after seeing that the front room was empty. In the store, dozens of clocks, hanging on the walls and sitting atop tables, chimed and ticked off the minutes. She walked up to the display case, filled with rings, bracelets, pendants, and all manner of glittering, sparkling jewelry, and listened.

After a moment, Robert tapped the service bell.

"Oh, just a moment," flavored with a Bavarian accent, a disembodied voice answered. Momentarily, an older man with thick, unruly, salt-and-pepper hair and a full beard to match whisked aside a curtain to the back office and hurried out. Smiling, he studied their faces as he approached the counter. "I know you. Miss Juliet." He offered her his hand. "Lovely to see you."

"Thank you, Mr. Mueller. This is my...friend, Mr. Robert Hall."

The two shook. "Mr. Hall. A pleasure."

"Likewise, sir."

"Well," Mr. Mueller dropped his hands to the counter. "How can I be of service?"

Juliet fished the locket from her reticule and handed it to the jeweler. "I think there is something in this locket. Something hidden."

His eyebrows launching to his hairline, Mr. Mueller popped open the locket. The photo fluttered out, and Juliet caught it, clasping it lightly. "It does that." She pointed at the piece of jewelry. "Look there in the back. We think we see the outline of something." The jeweler tilted the locket this way and that. "And if you run your finger over it, you can feel something. What do you think?"

Pulling a pair of eyeglasses from their hiding place in his chaotic tangle of hair, he settled them on the bridge of his nose. "Ah, I've seen this type of locket before."

"What do you think could be in there?"

He peered up at her over the tops of his spectacles. "People hide all kinds of things in lockets. Hair. Notes. Poison."

"Poison?" Robert said.

"Yah. All kinds of things. You wish me to open this locket?"

"Yes," Juliet said, nearly pouncing on the man.

Half-smiling, the jeweler pulled a small tool kit from his breast pocket and laid it and the locket on the counter. "It is a mystery, yes? How exciting." He pulled a small, L-shaped tool from the pouch, the tip of which ended in a sharp point. Slowly, carefully, he began to work it around the interior edge of the locket.

As he worked on it, Juliet caressed the photo of her husband. Robert didn't think she looked particularly sad, perhaps more thoughtful. "Angry or not, I suppose you miss him?" he asked.

She shrugged. "I didn't for a long time. For years, I just wanted to know what I didn't see, how I could have been so blind to this greedy, shallow side of him. I was angry with him *and* me." She flipped the photo over, almost absently, but stopped suddenly. Tilting her head a little, she brought the photo closer.

Robert leaned in. "See something?"

"Look." She showed it to him. "Luke 19:39-40. That's from the Bible, I think, but I don't know the verse."

"'And he answered and said unto them,'" Robert began, drawing both Juliet's and Mr. Mueller's gaze to him, "'I tell you that, if these should hold their peace, the stones would immediately cry out.'"

"That's right," Mr. Mueller agreed, going back to the locket.

"But what does that have to do with anything?" Juliet asked.

Robert looked at the locket. "Maybe everything. Maybe nothing."

The locket popped apart in Mr. Mueller's hands, and the small, oval backing clattered to the counter. "And there you go," he said, showing her the locket. "A key."

"A key." She lifted it out of the locket. A tiny, silver key, plain other than an engraving that read *FBN 223*. She glanced back and forth between the jeweler and Robert. "What does that mean?"

"Someone's initials?" Robert wondered aloud.

Juliet locked her gaze on Mr. Mueller. "My husband died saving this locket. Nearly got me killed. I need to know what it opens. Give me an idea."

The old man scrubbed his bushy chin. "Try the bank. If I had to guess, I'd say it opens a safe deposit box."

Chapter Four

Juliet double-timed it down the street, Robert at her side. She thought it seemed right somehow that he was here for this. Whatever *this* was. They skirted and side-stepped the traffic on the boardwalk as they made a beeline for the bank. Excitement flitted in her stomach and she could feel her lips trying to slip into a smile.

Finally, I might get my answer. And she couldn't keep her excitement to herself. "All these years, I thought he'd risked our necks for a twenty-dollar piece of gold jewelry. What if it's so much more? What if he was saving family heirlooms, or a secret fortune?"

"Is that all your lives were worth?"

Her step faltered. "N—No, I just meant that...that it wasn't petty greed. Or what if there is something truly valuable he was protecting? What if he was doing something good? And I've hated him all these years?"

Robert sucked in a deep breath and his face clouded over with a troubled look. She started to ask him if something was wrong, but the bank came into view and her excitement bubbled up all over again.

She grabbed his hand, surprised by the brash action, but

too giddy to worry about it. "Come on." They dashed across the street, dodging wagons and horses, and laughing over their adventure like a couple of children seeking buried treasure in the backyard.

———

Mr. Burns, the bank manager, lowered his magnifying glass and handed Juliet the key back across his desk. "That is to a safe deposit box at the First Bank of Nashville. Specifically, box 223."

Juliet settled back in her chair, turning the key over and over in her fingers, staring at it but not seeing it. Should she follow this mystery one more step? Of course. She couldn't stop now. She had to know. Know everything. She'd leave the bar in Sam's capable hands and head for Nashville tomorrow. Rash, perhaps, but she *had* to know.

Distracted, she thanked Mr. Burns, rose, and drifted out the door. Lost in her own thoughts, ambling down the walk, she slowly became aware of Robert again. "I have to go to Nashville," she said.

"I suspected as much."

"I'm going to leave tomorrow."

He nodded, dropping his hat back on his head, but didn't say anything. Instead, he regarded her with a questioning expression, as if he wanted to ask her something.

She put the key back in the locket, dropped it into her purse, then stopped and turned to him. "Something on your mind?"

He raised a hand to his hip, sucked air through his teeth, finally sighed. "Well, I'm on my way to Colorado. But a detour...for something so interesting..."

"You want to accompany me? Is that what you're getting at?"

He splayed out his hands in confession, giving her a bashful half-smile. "If you wouldn't—"

She started walking again and he had to scramble to stay with her. Juliet supposed there was no harm in it. Besides, it was always better to travel with a man for protection. She slid her gaze over to him. Was he trustworthy? He'd certainly spouted that Bible verse faster than a starving man grabbing for a steak. But did that mean anything?

She saw sinners *and* saints in her saloon every day. Men, in her experience, no matter how good they looked at first glance, turned out to be more sinner than anything else. All about their own needs. Waving the word *love* around as if it were a magic wand designed to open any and all doors.

"What sort of man are you, Mr. Hall?"

He took several steps with her before answering, his fingers laced behind his back. Juliet saw much of the military in his straight posture, as if he were still enlisted and waiting for a superior officer to walk up.

"I like to think I am an honorable man. I have a strong sense of justice..." He looked away, frowning. "Normally." But he straightened again. "I like to think I am the sort of man a woman can feel safe with."

"You saved me once," she half-mumbled.

He stopped and touched her sleeve. Again, she turned to him, and his iridescent blue eyes shimmered with sincerity. "And I would do it again. Preferably, I would take the arrow before it ever reached you."

His words left her speechless. Few men in the world were that noble. Most were liars. Juliet didn't think Robert Hall was most men. She had the unexpected desire to lightly trace her finger down the center of that curiously straight nose, then touch his lips. They seemed so inviting.

She took a small step back, shocked at herself. "I—I guess there's no harm in us taking the same train."

No, she hadn't meant to say that. She'd meant to say *go*

away. Don't waste my time. You're a liar. She couldn't seem to force any of those comments past her lips. Abruptly, she spun away and charged off down the walkway.

———

Robert had a clear responsibility to send a telegram to his superiors apprising them of the key and safe deposit box in Nashville.

He couldn't, however, get past a hesitation. A strong sense that he should *wait* before sending it. Puzzled, he sat down on the bed in his hotel room and laced his fingers in prayer.

Lord, if I send a telegram now, the department could choose to send a contact already in Nashville to check the contents of that safe deposit box.

He squeezed his eyes shut. *I don't think I should let that happen. I want to be the first one to see it. Or, more accurately, I want to be with Juliet when she sees what's in there.*

Why? Why does she matter so much?

Because...because all these years I've known I'd find her again. You said I would, Lord. I doubted You every now and then, but deep down, I knew Juliet was still out there. I can't believe You've had me hanging on to this feeling for her all these years just to find out she's a criminal. So I can arrest her?

What if that was My will?

Robert swallowed against the sting of the question. The possibility. *If she's guilty...if she's guilty of something...I will arrest her.*

He clenched his fingers into a tight fist. *I will do my duty. But something about this just doesn't feel right, Lord.*

Was he blinded by what a decade of hope had done to his ability to reason? He shook his head in disgust.

God, I've lost my way on this one. The assignment has become too personal. I guess it's always been too personal. But I believe Juliet is in danger— His eyes flew open. And he knew *that* was the truth, the reason behind his hesitation to blindly do his job. *Yes, she is in danger. Someone besides me has been looking for her for ten years. Otherwise, why was her file still open?*

Was it because of the locket?

Robert would send the telegram and tell his superiors about the locket, but not about the key. Not yet. He would tell them, using carefully worded half-truths, that they were going to a bank in Nashville. He wouldn't tell them about the safe deposit box, not until *after* he and Juliet had seen the contents.

And he would watch over her. No matter how this turned out for him, he would keep her safe.

Perhaps that was why he had hung on to his hope for ten years. Maybe love had nothing to do with his real purpose. Maybe God was asking him to merely do his job as a soldier.

And that might have to be good enough.

Chapter Five

Juliet started to put the locket away in her jewelry box, but leaned on her dresser instead and caressed the gold oval. So many questions and disconnected memories paraded through her mind.

She opened it and stared at her husband's face again. In ten years, she'd forgotten much, but the photo brought back some of it. They'd met in a wagon train of settlers headed for the Texas frontier. Juliet had been traveling with a family from New York. Hugh was leaving the war-torn South.

He was merely a worn-down-and-weary soldier for a lost cause, he'd told her. Before that, a simple teacher. He was going someplace where rules and laws were still being made. Where alliances and common goals were not yet muddied by politics. He wanted a hand in building a good place, a place where people lived free, politicians feared the voters, and wars weren't started for the benefit of the rich and powerful.

"If politicians suffered the consequences of a war, they'd hasten to end them, if they started them at all," he had told her once. *"The Civil War did not affect enough of them directly. Both sides were arrogant and disdainful of the sacrifices of good men."* And this was what passed as a tirade by the quiet, sensitive, former schoolteacher.

Not given to heated speeches—ever—he did freely express his particular loathing of the elected class.

She and Hugh had courted for a year in Rimfire, both of them knowing they would marry eventually. It had seemed inevitable. To Juliet, something about Hugh in her life was predestined.

Looking back, she could recall the feeling of certainty, but now not the passion behind it. Had there ever been any? A cruel question, but Hugh had been a man of thoughtful measures, thinking before he spoke, always dissecting, weighing, and considering situations.

He could be calculating, goal-oriented, a builder, a leader. But with very little...gusto. She had teased him for being a study in grim determination.

But he had made her feel safe. She could always count on him to do the wise thing, the pragmatic thing. Steady. Reliable. That was her Hugh. He had never exhibited overtly sentimental or foolish behavior. Even at the town gatherings, he had always been stone-cold sober, speaking in a measured tone, keenly aware of things around him. Conscious of his image and deportment. He had dreams of helping build Rimfire into something special, but he had no plans to run for office.

It seemed everything he had ever done, he'd done for a reason, but she'd never seen evidence of greed or materialism.

Until that day.

Frowning, she ran her finger over his face. *Did I misjudge you, Hugh? Misread you? All these years, were you trying to do something good? What secret does this locket hold?* She pulled his photo free and read the scripture reference again. *Why would the rocks cry out?*

No answer came forth from the long, cold trail of memories.

Chapter Six

Juliet delivered two cold ham biscuits and two beers to a couple of fellas in the corner, then resumed her station behind the crowded bar. She poured drink after drink, wiped up spills, chatted friendly-like with the usual patrons. Mostly a motley crew, they were river men, gamblers, salesmen, and cowboys headed down to Texas.

Sally's hit its stride around seven, and the place was crowded, loud, and smoky like this till midnight. She was taking off in a few minutes, though, at nine, to pack. The train pulled out at seven in the morning, and she planned on being early.

She'd half expected to see Robert again tonight. They'd parted after the bank with the agreement to meet at the station, but she'd thought he might come back for his drink.

The little, undeniable nudge of disappointment grated on her nerves.

As if alerted by some second sense, she glanced across the bustling, noisy room in time to see Robert pause at the bat wings and survey the crowd. Juliet waited for him to see her. Even through the haze, she caught the hint of something warm—almost tender—in his expression when his gaze found her.

Removing his hat, he nodded acknowledgment and sidled through the crowd, making his way to the bar. "A few hours do make a difference in this place," he said, laying the Stetson down on the counter. He slid two bits from his pocket and dropped the coin on the wood as well. "I'll take that drink now."

She reached for a bottle to her right while sliding the coin back to him. "Your money's no good here, Mr. Hall. Told you that. Far as I'm concerned, you've earned yourself an open tab for life in my place."

"That's too generous, Mrs. Watts."

"*And* you have to call me Juliet." She plunked a shot glass down in front of him and started pouring. "My house. My rules. You don't pay for anything, and you call me Juliet."

She pushed the drink toward him and waited with a twitchy little smile on her lips. *My, he has the bluest eyes I've ever seen. And that nose—so straight, you could use it as plumb line. Wonder who his people are? Scotch, I'd guess.*

He grinned and took the drink, his fingers brushing hers. "I thank you very kindly, Miss Juliet." He tossed the liquor back and whistled. "I don't drink much. Now I recall why."

She chuckled and grabbed a rag off the counter, returning his grin. The crowd jostled him a bit, and his hat looked to be in danger of turning into a water trough. She plucked it from the bar and placed it below.

Before she could rib him about not throwing his hat on the rack at the door, Mel Cannady shouldered his way brusquely up to the bar and slapped a sawbuck down in front of them. He was grimy and still a touch sweaty from his day's work. "I want a whole bottle, Miss Juliet. The boys and me worked hard today on the river."

Flinching slightly at the man's body odor, Robert pulled away from him. A little embarrassed at her clientele—something that had never bothered her before—Juliet took the money. "You could have washed up before coming in here. I would have appreciated it." She produced a bottle and four glasses from beneath the bar. "So, don't get rowdy. I'm not in the mood." She set them on the counter, none too gently, and then made his change. Handing him the bills, she waved a finger in his face. "I mean it, Mel. Behave yourself."

She wasn't fooling and he knew it. Juliet had her friendly tone and her I-took-an-arrow-in-the-chest-so-you-don't-scare-me tone. Most customers knew the difference and not to push her.

A bit humbled, the man nodded politely, mumbled a vague, "No, ma'am," and disappeared with his drink.

Robert seemed to mull over the situation for a moment with a dip in his brow. "You do command respect."

"I have to or I couldn't run this place." She reached behind her to untie her apron. "And I am done for the evening. I have to pack."

"Could I escort you home?" he blurted.

They both stared at each other. Because of his rushed tone, she couldn't decide what to make of the request, and Robert's wide blue eyes seemed to say he couldn't believe he'd had the audacity to make such a request.

She pointed skyward. "I live upstairs."

He glanced up at the balcony over their heads. "I'd still be happy to escort you. Perhaps you'd like a walk first?" He swallowed. "Fresh air. For some fresh air?"

An inner voice screamed at Juliet to head to her room, pack, go to bed. Stick with the plan. Yet, she heard herself say, "I'll get my wrap."

Chapter Seven

Ah, Millicent would never lose her fine looks. Senator Wilson enjoyed watching his *operative* sashay across his office, hips swinging in an inviting manner, bosom barely peeking over the lace of her conservative neckline. In the daytime, visiting his office, she had to be the unquestionable representation of a demure lady.

At night, well...she did as she was told. Always had.

She winked a glittering green eye at him and sat down. Her fiery red hair called to him, dared him to forget propriety and run his hands through it. Pull out those pins and let it spill. She smirked, as if she knew exactly what he was thinking.

His consort and most versatile asset for ten years now, the senator couldn't do without her. Wouldn't even try.

"Say something. You asked me here, remember?"

Senator Wilson cleared his throat. Business with her. Always business. "We found Maxwell's wife. She's in St. Joseph, still going by the name of Juliet Watts."

Millicent leaned forward. "Finally, a break."

"Taught us patience, though."

"Are you bringing her in or...?"

"I have an officer from the Bureau with this Juliet right

now, trying to find out what she knows, and I have a man watching them both. He's going to try to steal some evidence, a locket, but I want you to go to Nashville. The man from the Bureau says Mrs. Watts is going to a bank there. Find out why and try to beat them to whatever they're after.

"Nashville? I'll have to leave right now."

"My train is waiting."

She rose. "Is this it? We're finally going to be able to—"

"Bury any potential allegations. Bury the scandal and my connection to it for good." He rose as well and drifted around his desk to stand close to her. He let his stare cover every inch of her. "Play your cards right, Millicent, and you might finally make it to the White House as a resident, not the entertainment."

Apparently unable to subdue her excitement, she launched onto her toes and delivered a wet, hungry kiss to him. "*President* Wilson," she bit his lip.

Pain spiked in his mouth and he jerked away. Her bloodlust made her dangerous and so very inviting. He forgot the slight coppery taste in his mouth and laid his hands on her tiny waist.

"Curb your enthusiasm, sweets. Go to Nashville and see what you can find out. If you learn anything, send the telegram to the usual address."

She drifted her fingers up his chest to his string tie and tugged on it playfully. "Is the telegram on the train operational?"

"Yes."

"Good, I'll do a little investigating before I get to Nashville. I'll need every minute I can eke out."

———

Robert tried not to stare, but he couldn't get enough of looking at Juliet. After a decade, he'd been sure reality would not match up with his recollection or even his hopes. Yet, here Juliet Watts was, walking beside him on a dim, lightly populated walkway, and he was just as enamored with her as he had been ten years ago.

He forced himself to look up at the moon. Full, round, and white, beaming down on St. Joseph. In the distance, between two buildings, he caught the glimmer of moonlight on the Missouri River. If only this were a romantic encounter and not an investigation, he would suggest a walk by the water—

Movement in the shadows on the other side of the street drew his attention for a moment. When it didn't recur, he came back to his idea of a river walk. In fact, he was considering suggesting it when she asked, "What of you, Mr. Hall? Family? Wife and children somewhere?"

"No, ma'am." He felt her gaze.

"How is it such a catch as yourself hasn't been dragged to the altar?"

He didn't know what to make of her question. It almost sounded like a compliment, as if he were a prize yet to be won. "I'm not sure I understand your implication."

"You're a handsome man. Honorable—otherwise, you wouldn't have brought me the locket after all these years. Sounds as if you've had gainful employment, most likely will again when the gold fever passes. I can't understand the blinders on the women in your circle."

Robert shoved his hands into his pockets, fascinated by her assessment of him. Did he dare see her observation as a compliment? She made it sound so cold, so clinical. But her understanding of his circle wasn't right. He worked. All the time. He was never home. He was a pawn for the US Government. "My circle is work. I haven't had a lot of time for courting."

"In ten years, you couldn't find time? You must really like your job."

"Last month, we rounded up an entire gang of ne'er-do-wells that was robbing trains in Mississippi and East Texas. Left a trail of bodies behind them. Innocent folks. Yes, I like my job. Sometimes too much, I suppose."

"Do you mean to tell me you've never come close to marriage?"

He shrugged, recalling an auburn-haired Bostonian angel with eyes bluer than a September sky. If any woman could have turned him from the promise he was certain God had made him, Mary Kate would have been the one. "There have been a few close calls," he confessed, "but they weren't the right women."

Juliet smirked at, he knew, his use of *close calls*.

"You sound like all the men who wander into Sally's. Marriage is a prison. A jail cell. A life sentence."

"No, I only call them close calls because those young ladies would have been mistakes. They weren't what I was prom—uh, waiting for."

That seemed to intrigue her. She narrowed her eyes at him as she pulled her wrap tighter. "What are you waiting for? Or should I say *whom?*"

They took several steps before Robert had a carefully worded answer. "I met someone a long time ago." He spoke haltingly, wary of saying too much. "I've known for a while..." He trailed off. There was no way to explain this. He would sound foolish, lovesick. But the impression God had left him with—that *she* had left him with—was indelible. "I've known for a while that if I could wait, she would come back around. God asked me to trust Him." And He had written Juliet on Robert's heart.

"And how is that working out for you, Mr. Hall?" Her tone was sharp, even a little mocking.

"You have no time for God at all, do you?"

She grimaced. "And you're changing the subject."

"I am merely curious. You don't have to answer."

"Fine. I suppose I believe. I believe He is aloof, disconnected, and His love is tenuous at best. I believe He abandons you in your darkest hour." She stopped abruptly and turned to him, her head down, arms folded in front. "I should get home."

Robert snapped his mouth shut, deeply troubled by her vitriolic answer. "Of course." They started walking back the way they had come.

Still, one person's disbelief had never affected *his* belief. Where Robert was standing, with whom he was now strolling, was solid proof that God didn't make idle promises. "You asked how His plan is working out for me. I can tell you"—he smiled a little—"I think it's working just fine so far."

Chapter Eight

I think it's working just fine so far.

Juliet didn't know what to say to Robert's optimism. Not that it mattered. Robert had his God. Good for him. Probably helped shorten the lonely nights when he was curled up with a good horse waiting for bank robbers to ride by.

She'd had her...anger to keep warm. All these years, she'd kept her life separated from the world by using it and her disappointment in Hugh's betrayal as a fence. It struck her that she and Robert had this in common—their willingness to be alone.

What if her reason for living this way vanished? What if, all these years, she'd been wrong about Hugh? Oh, how the thought haunted her. "I didn't mean to pry or be disrespect-ful," she finally said. "No offense."

"None taken. I run into people every day who don't know the Lord like I do."

"I wonder how much I knew my husband. I won't lie. After all these years of thinking ill of him, I'm not sure how I'll feel if I find out he was actually selfless and heroic for reasons I can't fathom."

"How much did you know about him before you were married?"

"I was eighteen, Mr. Hall. I thought I knew everything about him that I needed to know."

Eighteen. What a babe I was. Innocent. Blind. Foolish.

"Do you think the key has something to do with his life before he met you or after? Could it be about a business deal he was making? I remember he was a businessman. Owned a mercantile, didn't he?"

Her mouth nearly fell open. "Your memory is very impressive, Mr. Hall."

"I really would like for you to call me Robert, if you're comfortable doing so, that is." His blue eyes drilled into her, to the point she could almost feel a caress.

"Robert then." She lowered her head and slowed her pace to think, to gather her wits. "I know he fought in the war. He was a teacher in North Carolina before that. He had a brother who was killed at Bull Run. No other relatives." She grasped her elbow and raised two fingers to her forehead. "He hated politicians. Said they were the scourge of the Republic." She shook her head. "So many years. I don't know. I'll keep thinking."

"On the train, I'll try to think of some questions. We'll make it a game of sorts. Maybe I'll ask the right thing and something will break loose."

"The gears in my brain will unfreeze?" She lifted a shoulder. "I suppose it will pass the time."

A moment later, they were in front of the Sally and she offered her hand for a goodbye. "Thank you for your company, Mist—I mean, Robert." He took her hand, and Juliet felt a spark of something suddenly heat the air between them. She barely managed to keep her face still. His grasp was warm and strong, comforting even. Undeniably, she liked the feel of his fingers wrapped around her hand. "And—and for the walk. I'll see you at the station."

He didn't let go. "I enjoyed this evening, Juliet. Thank you."

Juliet pulled free from his grasp and hurried inside the saloon, scolding herself for this warm, syrupy reaction to the man. *This is what comes of living alone for too long, Juliet. You...you can't control yourself. Take a deep breath and think about the locket. And the key.*

She let herself into her room lit with a low, dim lamp. Simply furnished. Comfortable. Her cave.

Yes, think about anything but Robert's broad shoulders or how easily you could reach out and drift your finger down that perfect nose of his to his lips. Don't think about the stray hair that keeps drifting across his forehead, begging to be brushed aside.

She leaned back against the door and repeated a mantra that was verging on a million repetitions—*love is a lie, and you can't get hurt if you don't fall into it.*

So, don't fall, Juliet. No matter what, don't fall.

Chapter Nine

Juliet didn't think sleep would ever come, but apparently it did. She knew because her eyes flew open and she couldn't recall why she had awakened. But the soft sound of metal tinkling and...someone breathing?

She held her breath and listened, her eyes carefully roaming over her shadowy bedroom. Her heart galloped in her chest, almost to a deafening clamor. Someone was in the room with her. There—over at her dresser—a man sifted slowly through her jewelry box. The moonlight was faint but he was tall, not very wide, and she could see he had longish, unruly hair. He wore a plaid shirt of indeterminate color, the suspenders of his breeches making a dark X on his back.

Her terror abruptly gave way to a sense of violation. It burst forth in her like a roiling caldron of rage. She flung back the covers and lunged for the man, murder in her mind. "Get out of my room! How dare you!"

The man whirled. Juliet saw the whites of his eyes jitter as his gaze leaped from her to the window behind her. *Oh, no you don't—*

She grabbed his shirt, intent on clinging to him like a baby opossum attached to its mother. "You're not going any—"

He pushed Juliet aside with a ferocious heave, sending her cartwheeling back to her bed. He leaped across her mattress and dove through the window in a shattering, screeching shower of glass. He landed on the balcony outside and hit the wood running, tearing off like the very hounds of hell were after him.

Absently aware of a faint odor, Juliet clambered to her feet and raced after him, but a sliver of glass sliced its way into her heel. She choked back a scream just as her door burst open in its own shower of wood from the busted frame. Her bartender, Sam, big and burly, massive sides of beef for hands, quickly surveyed the room and ran to Juliet.

"The window," she said, limping away from it and falling against him. "He went out the window. Find him."

Two other men had rushed in with him. "Creek, Hub," Sam ordered. "You boys look outside. See what you can find."

The two launched past them and out to the balcony as well. They split up, heading in opposite directions. Juliet knew they wouldn't find anything. The man had moved like lightning. He'd had no intention of staying to fight if he was discovered.

"Come on, let's get you to the bed so I can look at that foot, Miss Juliet."

She limped over and sat down, resting her back against the brass headboard. Sam lit the lamp, turned it up all the way, then peered at the cut, his old, grizzled face showing his concern with squinted eyes and thoughtful *umhmmms*.

"Not too bad, but I need to clean it and wrap it. Hub," he bellowed at the window. Momentarily, the short, quick-moving man reappeared in the window. "I changed my mind. Creek can keep looking. You bring me some bandages. I have some in the back room."

"Done." Hub dashed through the room and disappeared down the hall.

Sam sat at the end of Juliet's bed, her foot resting on his

leg, carefully wiping away the blood with his apron while she pondered the man going through her jewelry. Was this about the locket? She clutched it at her neck to make sure it was still there. Her bet was yes. If he hadn't found it in her box, would he have checked her next?

Would have been his last mistake.

"Hub," Sam hollered, jolting Juliet from her ruminations. "Hurry up with those bandages." He tossed the bloody apron to the floor and lifted her foot up again. "I don't see any glass in there. And it's not deep. Consider yourself fortunate."

Fortunate. She sighed, still furious that someone had had the audacity to try to rob her. But worse, she hadn't gotten in one good lick. She wasn't afraid of a fight. If the man hadn't caught her off balance, she would have fought him like a bobcat. As it was, she hadn't even gotten her claws into him. She was disappointed in herself, and the lack of an identification.

Who was the man?

Not Robert. That much she knew. She'd only gotten a quick glimpse, but she'd smelled him, too. Robert smelled like soap and leather, and something sweet, like apple pie, maybe. The thief had smelled like chewing tobacco, whiskey, and mud. Or rotten meat. Odors that permeated St. Joe and could describe half the men here.

"You don't have any idea who the fella was?"

"I don't think I know him. Nothing about him was familiar. But I might know who hired him?"

"Hired him?"

"I rounded up a special piece of jewelry, Sam. It kinda fell into my lap, you could say. Only three people know about, and I'm one of them. I seriously doubt Mr. Mueller would dispatch a thug to steal it. So that leaves—"

"The third man. The young fella I saw you with this evening?"

He'd brought it to her, thinking it was worthless. When he

discovered a clue hidden in it, he wanted it back, assuming he was about to lose some treasure.

The explanation was reasonable, but it didn't sit right with Juliet. It seemed too much of a departure from his character. Of course, she didn't know him that well. Hugh had proven you couldn't really ever know anyone. Regardless, Robert was the prime suspect, and she was going to have some choice words for him at the station in the morning. If he showed. Surely, he wouldn't. He'd have to know she suspected his involvement in the attempted robbery.

No, Robert Hall had high-tailed it out of St. Joe. And even now, after what had just happened, Juliet grudgingly admitted she was a little disappointed.

"Wasn't him," Sam said, taking the gauze from Hub and wrapping it around her foot.

"How do you know?"

The old man grinned, the wrinkles and sagging skin nearly forcing his eyes shut. "He might steal something all right, but it won't be your jewelry."

"Don't say that, Sam. I don't have time—"

"You're not getting any younger, little girl. And you can't keep hiding out in this saloon. There's a whole lot of world out there waiting on you." He finished the bandage and tied it neatly with a bow. "I've been praying something would snap you out of your funk. Maybe this piece of jewelry and the Third Man are it."

Juliet lifted her foot and slipped it back under the covers. "I want to go to sleep now, Sam. Thank you for tending to me."

"Ah," he huffed and stood up. "It's all right. Stay off it as much as you can for a day or two."

"That won't be hard since I'll be on a train for the next couple of days."

"He going with you?"

"I told him he could, but now I'm not so sure if he should."

"Well, if I'm wrong about him—and I don't think I am—Machiavelli said, 'Before all else, be armed.' You armed?"

"I will be."

Chapter Ten

"How stupid do you think I am?"

The small-boned fist roared out of the dawn's gloom and hit Robert's jaw with the force of a shovel swung by a much larger man. Vision blurring, his brain fogging, he staggered back away from Juliet, holding his face. His hat tumbled to the ground behind him.

She stepped toward him, one hand clutching her suitcase, the other flexing over and over as if the punch had hurt her as well. Her pinched lips and burning eyes said she was ready to throw another, regardless of the passengers on the platform eyeing her with mouths agape.

"You try to rob me and then show up here to ride the train with me?"

Robert couldn't fathom what was causing this outburst. "I don't think you're stupid at all," he said, working his jaw back and forth. "And maybe if you tell me what's got you so riled, I can explain. Who tried to rob you?"

"Like you don't know."

"I *don't* know."

She narrowed her eyes at him, slivers of cold fire shooting from them. "Someone was in my room last night rifling through my jewelry. *Jewelry*. Clearly, he was after the locket. *I haven't told anyone about it.*" She raised her eyebrows in accusation at him.

"I didn't tell anyone." But he had. He'd sent a telegram. Making sure the revelation didn't show on his face, he said, "Perhaps Mr. Mueller told someone. Innocently enough. He told the wrong person, or the wrong person overheard?"

Her gaze narrowed down to slits of jade. Robert raised his hands in surrender. "If I had tried to rob you, Juliet, would I be here now?"

"Yes. Because you can play dumb. You're here because you want to know what that key opens."

"Absolutely. I do. I don't deny it. I'm on fire with curiosity. Harmless, simple curiosity."

She glared at him. He refused to wither beneath it. After a moment, she whirled away. "You show up ten years later with a locket I never wanted to see again, and now suddenly people are breaking into my room, and I don't think I knew my husband. Something here is all wrong."

"I agree." More than she could know. "Juliet"—he stepped closer to her—"you have no reason to believe this, but you *can* trust me. I won't do you any harm. I swear it." He wanted to tell her he'd do anything to protect her, but such a declaration certainly wouldn't *sound* like simple, harmless curiosity.

The train whistled and the conductor appeared at the entrance to the first car, watch in hand. "Now boarding, folks, for St. Louis." The whistle blew again. "Aaaaaall aboard," he sang. "St. Louis and points east."

Robert hated this. Juliet had every right to be suspicious of him. Someone had done great harm to the delicate trust they'd built. He was angry and wanted answers about this betrayal. Someone at the Bureau was meddling in this investigation. They wanted the intelligence before Robert had a chance to analyze it. Someone was afraid of what that key might unlock, and Juliet had no idea what was whirling around her.

"Who broke into my room?"

"I swear I don't know."

"I don't believe you," she said, turning back to him. She regarded him with a stony expression, but he'd heard the disappointment in her voice.

"And that grieves me more than I can say, Juliet."

She dropped her gaze to the ground, thinking, debating?

"Juliet, you won't be sorry if you let me come with you."

She sighed, and he prayed it was the sound of surrender.

She looked up. "It's out of your way. The opposite direction from Colorado."

"It's a detour. Colorado isn't going anywhere."

"But the gold is. Into someone else's pockets."

"I'll find what I'm meant to find."

"It's your loss then."

"Maybe."

————

Robert had no idea if he had an invitation to sit with Juliet, but when she sat and glared up at him with an I-dare-you expression, he had his answer. Still, he would not be deterred that easily. He needed to question her about the man who had broken into her room.

The seating on the train featured one section of all forward-facing benches, and then a lesser number of benches that were grouped facing each other. She had chosen to sit in one of these. Hat pressed to his chest, Robert moved to the next seat, which had him sitting with his back to her—not how he had envisioned their seating arrangement. He would have sat across from her, but there was a male passenger there already, stretched out and lounging, taking up the whole bench. Sucking through his teeth, Robert knew this arrangement would make communication difficult, but not impossible.

And he had time. He set his hat down beside him. This was a long, slow, monotonous train ride across the heart of the country. Surely, she'd want conversation...in time.

Not wanting to be rude, he exchanged pleasantries with a matronly-looking woman who settled across from him with her picnic basket and bag full of yarn. Several minutes later, the train whistled again and rolled out of St. Joe, steam hissing and wheels clacking.

The faster the train went, the more Robert's fellow passenger seemed to desire conversation. A retired teacher, Mrs. Welch was headed to St. Louis to visit her grandchildren. All ten of them. Robert pretended to be interested, nodding politely, but was trying to listen to Juliet pass a few words with the male passenger sitting opposite her. Her tone was cool, not cordial. Arguably disdainful. The man didn't seem to notice and babbled on about the cattle business, Indian attacks out in Nebraska, and scandals in Washington.

An hour out of St. Joe, Robert turned his head a little and made his first attempt at small talk. "I understand we'll stop in Independence, long enough for lunch. I'm pretty hungry. What about you?"

She sniffed. "Not very."

Rebuffed, but not defeated, he smiled sheepishly at Mrs. Welch, who was fighting a smile. Juliet had spoken softly but not with any warmth, and the older woman had clearly heard the exchange. Embarrassed, not to mention a touch annoyed, Robert rested his hands on his knees and drummed his fingers.

Mrs. Welch reached out and tapped him on the leg. Startled, he looked up. She shooshed her hand at him in a get-going motion and mouthed, *go sit with her*. She followed up the advice with a wink and a grin. "I was married sixty-three years, son," she whispered. "Sometimes, you've just got to push past their pride."

Robert's cheeks flushed. Total strangers were giving him advice on his love life.

What love life?

He shifted uncomfortably in the seat, but Mrs. Welsh was still grinning. Truthfully, maybe she was telling him just what he needed to hear.

Well, I am more than a conqueror through Christ.

He flinched, sorry for the flippancy. *Lord, I could use Your help about now. Juliet is...a challenge.* One, he hoped, he was up to.

Resolved, he rose to his feet, turned, and stepped to the opening between her bench and the male passenger, who still had his legs sprawled out, practically blocking all the space in front of Juliet. Robert wasn't about to step over the man who clearly needed a lesson in manners. When he looked up, Robert speared him with a not-too-pleased glare rich with promise. Apparently, the man didn't want any trouble and pulled his legs in. Robert stepped past him and sat down beside Juliet.

"So, I've been thinking—"

"Good for you," she interrupted, turning slightly away from him and folding her arms across her ribs.

All right, fine. If she was going to play some stubborn, petulant princess, so be it. It wouldn't change the fact that he had a job to do, which included protecting her. "Tell me every-thing you can recall about the man who broke into your room. Tell me exactly what he was doing when you woke up, anything you remember about him, anything at all."

She let out a soft, but exasperated breath and didn't answer. Robert tried to tamp down his temper. He understood her hesitancy in not trusting him, but they had to get past it. "Juliet, I told you I've been involved in...law enforcement," he said carefully. "Let me...do my job. Let me help you."

She didn't move. Didn't breathe. Shortly, though, she swiveled on the seat to face him more directly. "His hair was rather long. To his shoulders is my best recollection. It was brown, I think, but it was dark in my room." She worked her jaw back and forth. "And he smelled. Like..." She trailed off and spent a good several seconds trying to find the perfect match. "Spoiled meat. It wasn't overbearing. It was there, though."

"Spoiled meat?" He puzzled over that for a moment. A hunter? Or a skinner? Often those men were a rough lot and willing to hire out for less-than-savory assignments. "Did he say anything?"

"Nothing."

"When you first discovered him in your room, what was he doing exactly?"

"Going through my jewelry box."

Well, that was hard to see in any light other than the obvious. "Then you are right to assume he was after the locket." Therefore, the man was probably hired by someone in the Bureau, which meant the break-in did indeed tie directly back to her husband. "Let's come at this from a different angle. Tell me about Hugh Watts. He served in the war? What side? How did he serve? In what capacity?" Robert knew what he'd read. He knew what the Bureau suspected. What had Hugh told his own wife?

"He fought for the South. Served in the Alabama 53rd. He said he was a second lieutenant. Something with the cavalry, as best I recall, but he rarely talked about it."

Robert leaned back on the bench, stared up at the ceiling of polished pine slats. A lamp swung overhead, in time with the click-clack rhythm of the train. "Did he mention any names from the war? Did he keep in touch with any of his comrades?"

"No." Shaking her head, Juliet pulled her long, golden hair around and began to braid it. "We talked of the war one time. His unit was ordered to guard a train of what they thought was ammunition and cannons. He discovered, instead, they were taking a Union officer from Richmond to Charleston to meet with Jefferson Davis—"

"A sympathizer in the ranks?"

"So Hugh said. The train was attacked somewhere in North Carolina. To get the officer away safe, the rebels blew a bridge, killing dozens of soldiers."

The revelation of a spy in Grant's cadre had Robert reeling. "Did he say who was on the train?"

"No. I asked. He said I wouldn't know the name. The event...demoralized him, I believe. And it wasn't the only time he saw soldiers used as pawns. He thought it mightily unfair the way the rich and the powerful could orchestrate such a conflict and not be affected by it. Worse, they benefited from it. He said the abuse of power that sent boys to their deaths was more evil than the battles themselves."

"He sounds like a man with a strong sense of honor." Which made Robert wonder why he would have become a traitor and order so many men to their deaths.

Juliet's hands paused while braiding. "His loathing of all things political was the only matter that ever got him to raise his voice. Hugh was a quiet man, deliberate, reserved. He was very purposeful in everything he undertook." She shifted her gaze to Robert, and for an instant, he was lost in her eyes, magical, mystical shimmering jade. "I believed he loved me. He made me feel safe and gave me such hope for our future. But I always sensed he was driven by something. I assumed it was ambition. That made it easy to believe he wanted the locket because of its value, not its worth, if you understand the difference."

"I think so."

She wagged her head slightly but said nothing else. Robert pondered her assessment of Hugh/Maxwell. She hadn't mentioned anything that he thought was of much help, though a sketch of the man's personality might be useful eventually. He scratched his nose and decided to piece together the time-line. "When did he get you the locket?"

She thought for a moment. "After we'd been in Rimfire a few months. I remember thinking at the time it was strange of him to give me a gift for no apparent reason. It wasn't my birthday, and we weren't engaged yet."

"Did you ask him why?"

"Yes. He said he just thought I'd like to have it and"—she paused and let a small smile break—"he wanted me to know he trusted me with his heart. Looking back, of course it seems odd. He was not given to random acts of affection. I excused it as...a man in love." The smile faded as her obvious doubts replaced it.

With every conversation, Robert became more and more convinced that Juliet had no idea of her husband's traitorous activities during the war. At the same time, his curiosity about the key in the locket, all the secrets it might unlock, burned in him like proverbial gold fever. He regretted, however, that the truth about Hugh's past would snuff Juliet's growing hope that she had been wrong about her husband, that he'd saved the locket for some altruistic reason.

On the surface, it looked like Hugh/Maxwell had chosen to sacrifice lives on that bridge in North Carolina so he could spirit the mysterious VIP to safety. Clearly, though, he hadn't explained the situation that way to Juliet. The dossier at the Bureau did not give the mystery man's name or his importance to the Confederacy. Maybe the locket would. Robert would follow the clues all the way to the end to find out. He suspected, so would Juliet.

Chapter Eleven

Juliet stared out the window at the acres of withering, spindly corn awash in the orange hues of sunset. This corner of Southern Illinois was in desperate need of rain. The fall harvest had to have more than a few farmers worried, she judged by the condition of the crops.

Her head hurt from trying to figure out what Hugh was hiding. What kind of a man had he been, really? She hoped she was wrong about him. She would rather know he died for a reason other than greed than live with this anger and betrayal anymore. She'd been undone by it. Left drifting. Removed from God. So alone. But she couldn't let go, couldn't forgive—Hugh or God—until she knew the truth.

Which begged the question, what if she discovered all of this *was* over a trinket? That Hugh had simply been shallow and greedy. God *was* removed from the cares of His children, watching in boredom as they stumbled along from one random disaster to another. The thought left her hopeless and chilled to the bone. She wanted hope. She wanted to believe love was real.

"A penny for your thoughts."

Startled, she looked up at Robert. In spite of her dark musings, something fluttered to life inside her at the sight of him. His strong, proud nose, those piercing blue eyes, the way his golden blond hair fell across his forehead gave her an unbidden sense of *comfort*. He smiled, and the action caused his crow's feet to deepen, adding maturity and wisdom to a face she already liked. But was he friend or foe? She didn't trust him. Wouldn't let herself.

He sat down beside her again, back from chatting with the conductor. "We'll be in Pittsboro in another hour. Just in time for a steak dinner. Hungry yet?"

She decided not to lie. "Famished."

"You should have gone to lunch earlier. It was rather enjoyable. Mrs. Welch had some very entertaining stories about her years as a teacher."

"Don't let him fool you, dear," Mrs. Welch said, gliding by them, apparently headed for the ladies' room. "He was polite, but his mind was elsewhere."

Robert's jaw tightened, puzzling Juliet. She turned her head slightly, waiting for Mrs. Welch to fade from earshot. When the woman was several feet down the row, Juliet leaned forward a touch. "I was sitting here wondering what I'll do if the key tells me what I already know. Or think I know."

"What do you think you know?"

"That Hugh died because he was simply greedy, and God really couldn't care less."

Robert's expression softened to the point that he looked almost pained by her confession. She both despised him for the pity she saw there and appreciated the compassion. What a strange mix of emotions he brewed in her. But she had told him her thoughts because, oddly, she thought he might have an answer, some words of wisdom.

"You think," he started as he laced his fingers together and rested his hands between his knees. "You think Hugh's death was random?" he shrugged a shoulder, "And there's no point to anything because God can't be bothered with us?"

Juliet leaned her head back on the seat. "Random? No, but pointless. He *chose* to risk our life together, my life, for his purpose. That's not love. And God allowed it. Stood by and let those brutal Indians..." She didn't finish.

"Allow me, if you will, to share a story."

She motioned to her surroundings. "I'm a captive audience."

He chuckled at her sarcasm. "Not long after I enlisted, I was assigned to an artillery unit in Maryland. A quiet, unassuming young Irishman served with us. Sean Flynn. I'll never forget him.

"He seemed a good sort. Quiet, hard-working, but he was small in stature. I didn't make much of an effort to get to know him, as I had already become friends with three or four of the other men in the unit. Oh, Sean and I talked some, but I didn't exactly overwork myself to get to know him."

Juliet sat quietly, but didn't bother to hide her growing boredom.

"One afternoon, Sean and I were ordered to go into town to pick up supplies. We made our rounds, got the wagon loaded, then decided to wet our whistles at the local saloon before heading back.

"Well, we were sitting there, minding our own business, me keeping the conversation going because Sean didn't say much, when I allowed I'd like a snack before we left. So, I go up to the bar to purchase two boiled eggs. Well, a handful of pretty belligerent drunks come stumbling in while I'm talking to the bartender. One thing led to another, and before I had time to spit, I was in the middle of a fight." Robert moved to the edge of his seat. "My head gets knocked back on my shoulders, bells are ringing in my ears, and I'm thinking to myself, *I am going to go back to the fort with all manner of injuries, and how am I going to explain that to the captain?*

"But before I could right myself and throw a single punch, Sean comes flying into the fray like a crazed whirling dervish. Fists flying, curses streaming," Juliet smiled at Robert's wild boxing gestures and enthusiasm for the story. "He laid those boys out faster than a hawk pouncing on a cold rattlesnake."

"My," she said flatly.

Robert settled back a little. "I'd never seen anything like it." He shook his head, still incredulous. "Haven't to this day." He shifted forward again, signaling his continual enthusiasm for the story. "Stunned and amazed at the little man's ferociousness, I said to Sean, 'Sean, of all the men at the fort I would have thought could save my hide, well, honestly, you wouldn't have come to mind first." Robert leaned a little closer to Juliet. "The Irishman, rubbing his knuckles, looks up at me, a mischievous twinkle in his eyes, and says"—Robert put on Irish accent for this—"'Boyo, there's a lot ye dooon't knoooow about me. Ye've no idea what I'm capable of.'"

A triumphant expression on his face, he settled back, as if satisfied he'd made a profound point. But he wasn't done. "Here's the punch line. On the way back to camp, Flynn explained to me that he'd come from a family of boxers and brawlers. By the time he left Ireland, he'd held the national title. Twice. But he'd been dethroned by a cousin."

Juliet nodded, but it drifted into a confused shaking of her head. "Your point to this fascinating story is...?"

"If I'd bothered to get to know Sean Flynn before that day, I would have had a hint of what he could do." He shifted to face her more fully. "You don't know what God can do, Juliet. You don't have a clue about what He thinks, the how or *why* of His plans for you, if He can move your mountains or not, because you haven't spent any time with Him. You've made assumptions, but you haven't gotten to *know* Him."

Suddenly Juliet felt remiss—even embarrassed—as if she'd let some important opportunity slip by. Not much of a believer before Hugh's death, she couldn't see wasting her time on God after...but Robert's story—surprisingly—did make her wonder. Assumptions were, indeed, dangerous things. Trumpeters of lazy thought.

"The first thing you should know is He loves you."

The words weighed on Juliet's heart, troubling her. Or perhaps she was just affected by Robert's charming, almost hypnotic storytelling and tender gaze.

The corner of his mouth lifted in a half-smile. "How could He not?"

She felt her eyes widen. Her breath caught in her chest. Robert's words made her heart beat a little faster, but he blinked and looked away quickly, as if embarrassed by the sentiment. Puzzled and a little flustered, Juliet shifted her own gaze out the window to the wilted corn passing by. Ten years of being alone had left her vulnerable to tender expressions. Had softened her recollection of the hard lesson learned in Rimfire.

Well, pretty words and promises are just disguised lies, the biggest one of which was called Love.

———

Butterflies cavorting in her stomach, Juliet watched Robert build the fire at their little campsite in the rolling hills of Tennessee. She hadn't slept out in the open since she'd taken the wagon train to Texas a decade ago. The scent of smoldering hickory filled the air. The back of their campsite nestled up against a row of towering southern pines, and in front of them, a strikingly green pasture flowed down and off to the west. A small brook babbled just on the edge of the tree line, and overhead, the last orange and red streaks of sunset were fading away. Robert had found them a beautiful spot to spend the night. Alone. Just the two of them. The butterflies surged again.

Switching trains in Union City, a fellow passenger had overheard her and Robert discussing the route to Nashville. He had confidently advised them of a faster way to get there. A traveling salesman, he suggested they skip one leg of the train ride and take the stage straight from Union City to Clarksville, pick up the train again there. His route, he said, would shave one whole day off their journey.

However, upon inquiring at the Wells-Fargo line, they learned the stage had already departed. The young boy at the window, assuming Robert and Juliet were married, said off-handedly they could rent a wagon if they were in such an all-fired hurry. They still had plenty of daylight left to make a start.

Robert and Juliet's eyes had met, and she'd nodded slightly. Why wait?

An hour later, they rode out of Union City, and at dusk, he chose this campsite. The fire going strong, he strode to the back of the wagon and pulled a blanket from the back, a canteen, and two boxes. "If you'll hold these," he handed her everything but the blanket, which he spread out on the ground. "Now..." He took one of the boxes from her and the canteen from her. "I'm ready to eat. How 'bout you?"

He sat down, removing and setting his hat on the blanket, and she dropped down beside him. Together, they opened the boxes. Juliet was surprised, delighted, in fact, to see a biscuit and two fried chicken legs inside hers. "When did you get this?"

"A café next to the livery. We should be in Clarksville by mid-morning, but I wasn't inclined to go without supper tonight if I didn't have to."

She took a bite of the chicken and was immeasurably glad he'd thought this far ahead. "Thank you." A lightning bug floated past and, gasping, she realized the entire field was coming to life with them. "Look at that." Fairy-like points of light flitted, winked, and drifted all over the pasture. Shortly, the crickets started, a comforting summer serenade, adding a beautiful song to the picture before them. "It's beautiful here."

He studied the scene with a little smile. "My favorite time of day, especially in the summer. It truly shows what an artist God is."

She thought again of Sean Flynn and the lesson Robert had shared. No, she didn't know God the way she should, but maybe there was time—

A lightning bug landed on her knee and she watched it for a moment, his little body glowing intermittently. And then he was off again, flying, drifting, searching for love in the summer night.

Two thoughts struck her at once: the beauty of the evening, the *wonder* of it...and, again, that she was alone with Robert. She became aware of him for the millionth time that day, how close he was now, his scent of sweat, and leather, and *him*. Her heart sped up a little, her breathing quickened. There was no one here to watch them, cast curious glances their way, try to talk to them. They were alone and her heart tripped over itself.

What was the matter with her? She was being ridiculous. "Could you pass me the canteen?"

"Certainly." He did, and their fingers touched. For an instant, their eyes met and his seemed to flicker with a hypnotic light. Slowly, she pulled the canteen away and took a sip.

"Besides being a mortician, my father was also a farmer." He had a strange wiggle in his voice and cleared his throat. "My two brothers still work the farm, just outside Sheffield. I visit when I can. It's pretty country." He nodded at the field on the other side of the fire. "This reminds me of it."

"Do you miss it?"

"I had a good boyhood there. Swimming in our pond in the summer, hay rides in the fall. The winters were relentless, though, and made a young man with adventure on his mind chafe." He looked down and put his unfinished chicken back in the box. "I regret that I so easily walked away from my family. It seems to get harder and harder to make time to visit. My career calls me away often." He stiffened a little, as if he'd said something he shouldn't, and Juliet's interest was piqued.

She put the remnants of a chicken leg back in her box and set it aside. "What is it that you do in law enforcement? Or did? Why did you leave it for prospecting? That's risky."

"I've done some"—he shrugged and dragged out his answer —"*work* tracking down bank robbers and such. I ride along with posses more than anything. The prospecting is temporary. The fever will pass. I'll most likely go back into the law in some way."

Juliet sniffed. "That makes more sense than what I hear from the men who come through the saloon. They're convinced they're going to strike it rich in three days and retire." She looked out over the field alive with the fireflies. "Fools."

Robert shook his head. "Juliet, were you always this...?"

"Bitter? Angry?"

"I was going to say pragmatic."

Heat rushed her cheeks. "Oh." She picked up his hat and put it on, purely as a delay tactic. "My bartender Sam tells me I hold on to grudges and that I should learn to let things go. He thinks I'm angry."

"Maybe you won't be when we get to the end of this."

Juliet hugged her knees to her chest and rested her chin on them. She didn't know what to say to that. Letting go of her hard feelings toward Hugh seemed impossible at the moment. She'd lived on the bitterness for so long.

Unexpectedly, another sound filtered in with the crickets and she lifted her head. "Do you hear that?"

A fiddle and a banjo, faint but clear, drifted to them on the warm breeze. They listened for a few minutes, enjoying the jaunty version of "Dixie." "Must be a house nearby," Robert said, "or maybe an inn up the road."

Juliet had to laugh. "Watch there be a fine establishment

just around the curve. We could have had a hot meal, a hot bath, and a soft bed to sleep in if we'd gone another hundred yards."

"Is this so bad?" he asked softly. Her stomach fluttered—not unpleasantly—beneath his gaze, made more alluring by the fire's flickering light.

"No...I guess not," she said, sounding too breathy.

"Juliet, would you dance with me?"

The music had softened and slowed to her favorite song, "Beautiful Dreamer." Robert didn't wait for an answer. He took her hands in his and pulled her to her feet. He slipped his arm around her waist, but didn't pull her too close. Juliet was mystified by how wonderful her hand felt in his, how natural it was to rest her palm on his shoulder, to *touch* him. His fingers caressed the small of her back, and his eyes held hers as they took slow, awkward steps on the blanket.

Something in Juliet changed. It almost felt like...she struggled to understand it...a softening? A melting? No man had held her like this since Hugh's death. Slowly, Robert pulled her to him. Her body pressed against his. Heat like a furnace radiated from him, or was she radiating the heat? He smiled slightly, pensively, as if he thought a bigger smile might scare her away.

And she was scared. What was happening? Her face was only an inch or two from his, their lips were so close, so magnetic. Their breath mingled. Hypnotized. Entranced. Bewitched. All words that went through her mind as she imagined kissing Robert.

Kissing him?

The song ended and the breeze died. They stood frozen, silent, the crickets the only sound. Juliet blinked and this fog, this magic spell, ended. She swallowed and stepped back. She was so foolish, so weak and wavering. But she couldn't find it within herself to be angry—with either of them. "I'm going to bed now. Thank you for the dance."

Robert licked his lips. "My pleasure." He pointed at the wagon. "You sleep in there. I'll take the ground."

She nodded, but her feet didn't move at first. Now the anger flared. *You're being ridiculous, Juliet.*

Properly chastised, she went to the wagon but knew sleep would be a long time coming.

Chapter Twelve

Juliet wondered if it was a prerequisite for bank managers to grow barrel-chested, wear tiny, gold-rimmed spectacles, and sport bushy beards. If so, Mr. Jack Fenton was an obedient soul. He greeted her and Robert in the lobby of the First Bank of Nashville with a wide grin and outstretched hand.

"Good afternoon. I'm Jack Fenton, the manager."

"Mrs. Juliet Watts. My attorney—" she motioned to Robert, who stepped forward and offered his hand, "Mr. Robert Hall."

The manager's eyes rose a little. "What can I do for you, Mrs. *Watts*, was it?"

He seemed almost troubled by the name, but Juliet didn't stop to question him. "I'd like to get into my husband's safe deposit box, please. He's deceased."

"I see." He dragged out his words, as if puzzling over something. "You have the key, or shall I—?"

"I have it." She pulled it from her reticule, wondering why he didn't offer condolences for her loss.

His bushy beard twitched. "All right." Only he didn't sound as if he thought things were all right at all. A crease betraying worry appeared in his forehead. "If you'll follow me, please." They entered a room roughly fifteen feet by fifteen feet, the walls of which were lined with dozens of small, numbered doors. A table and two chairs sat in the center. "Your key, Mrs. Watts, and I'll pull the box out for you." She handed it to him, and the banker's face twitched at the number, first in surprise, then suspicion.

He looked at Juliet over the top of his spectacles, then back to the item in his hand. Frowning, he raised his chin as if readying for a fight. "I'm afraid I don't understand. Mr. Watts's *wife* was by here this morning. I thought perhaps your name was an odd coincidence, but she asked to see his safe deposit box, too. *This* safe deposit box."

Juliet and Robert exchanged shocked glances. She leaned into the banker. "I'm the one who doesn't understand. *I'm* Hugh Watts's wife. He doesn't have another wife, and he's been dead for ten years."

He couldn't have another wife. The possibility sickened her, made the floor roll beneath her feet.

Sweat popped out on the banker's lip. "Madam, she said her name was Juliet Watts and that she was the wife of the deceased owner. She was listed as the co-signer."

"But I'm Juliet Watts. She has to be a phony."

"I am a gentleman, Mrs. Watts. I had no reason to doubt her word."

Robert inched forward. "You *should* have doubted, and you should have asked for identification."

"Well, I—" Mr. Fenton tapped his silk tie, his perplexed expression switching to a more stubborn hue. "You misunderstand. She did not have proper identification but said she would get it and return. As of yet, she has not. Therefore, I, of course, need to ask you for identification," he said to Juliet, "and that might end this confusion."

Juliet's lips slipped into a tight, thin line. "I have my marriage license with me. And the death certificate. That should suffice?"

"Well, I-I. Yes, yes, of course," Mr. Fenton stuttered.

Robert touched the banker on the shoulder. "Can you recall what this other Mrs. Watts looked like?"

"She—she was quite attractive. Stunning, you could say. A brunette, I believe. Slender. Taller than Mrs. Watts here. A southern accent, and—oh, I remember we discussed peaches." His look of triumph at remembering something more specific wilted under their glares. "Mrs. Watts, if you'll show me your marriage certificate, please..."

Robert fished it from his satchel he had tucked beneath his arm and handed it over.

Mr. Fenton grunted after a review and returned it, his now humble gaze settled on Juliet. "My apologies. I can't imagine who this other woman was or what she was after. Clearly, there is something awry here. We'll have the matter investigated at once." He swallowed, the sound pronounced in the small room.

"So, she did not gain access to the safe deposit box or any of Hugh's accounts?" Juliet asked.

"No, madam."

Robert gently but firmly backed the banker to the door. "Mrs. Watts will be closing her husband's accounts, if there are any. I have a copy of the will with me, as well as the death certificate. If you'll be so kind as to start the paperwork, we'll be along."

"Of course." He handed the key back to Juliet. "I believe the other Mrs. Watts—uh, I mean, yes, the other wom—she meant to close the accounts as well, but of course, that was out of the question without proper identification."

"How fortunate for me."

Mr. Fenton didn't respond, only slunk from the room like a chastised dog.

Robert waited for the man to leave, then scanned the walls of boxes, and after a moment pulled a long, cylindrical container from a bottom row on the back wall. "There you go."

He set it on the table, but Juliet merely stared at it. "Did he have another wife? Did he divorce her? Or abandon her?" A horrible thought struck her. "Or neither. What if he had a relationship with her somehow while—?"

"I don't think she was his wife, Juliet."

"How do you know that?"

"I don't *know* it, but it feels wrong. I told you, I have some law enforcement background. Whoever she was, I think she was just supposed to get to Hugh's affairs." He nudged the box toward her. "Maybe you'll find some answers in there."

Clamping her jaw, Juliet inserted the key, heard a click, and lifted the lid. For a moment, she and Robert merely stared in silence.

Chapter Thirteen

The first thing Juliet saw was the photo of Hugh...in a *Union* uniform. Her breathing shortened to little snatches of air and her heartbeat thrummed in her ears. *In the Union army? He did lie to me.*

This was an induction photo, usually taken by families sometime not long after enlistment. Hugh was young, had more hair, more meat on his bones, and wore the bars of a second lieutenant. He stood erect, proud, holding his rifle at his hip.

"I don't understand." She picked up the photo, tried to swallow her fear, her disillusionment. "He said he fought for the South." *Why the lies?*

For a moment, Robert regarded her with pity. Yes, she could see it clearly in his face. Poor, innocent, naive Juliet. Had believed every word Hugh had told her. For whatever reason, most likely to hide some betrayal or cowardice, he had hidden the truth of his past. Had he abandoned a young wife? Sought refuge in the South? Had he disagreed with Northern aggression?

Yet, he had never spoken up for slavery. To her recollection, he had never defended the South—he'd only ever mentioned his support of state's rights, his aversion to over-reaching government...

"Look at this." Robert reached into the box and pulled out another photo. "This is the one in the locket."

Hands trembling—she didn't know if from fear or disappointment—she took the photo from him. Uncropped, this picture held much more detail than the one in the locket. Hugh, older here, stood in the foreground of the photo—an encampment. Off to one side, she saw a tent, a fire, tack and saddles sitting on the ground, horses tied to a picket line. Possibly the crumbling remnants of an old stone chimney.

She was surprised to see that Hugh was not alone. Two other men stood in the background, off to his right. One held an axe, the other a handsaw. All of the men were dressed in random fragments of Army uniforms. Hugh wore a Confederate officer's jacket, the other two men wore dark pants from a Union soldier's uniform. One also sported a gray kepi with sergeant stripes on it.

"And look at the background."

In the far distance, tall, saw-tooth mountains cut the sky. This photo was not taken anywhere in the eastern United States. Where then? "I don't understand any of this." She held the photos side by side. "Was he running from a bad marriage? Did he or didn't he fight for the South? Did he—" Another horrible thought stabbed her in the heart. "Was he a traitor? Or a spy? For which side?" Her knees buckled and she dropped into the chair, her bustle making a soft thud. She held on to the pictures.

"You honestly don't know, do you?"

She closed her eyes, humiliated. "No. It would make more sense if he were a spy for the North, but I don't know anything anymore. The way he went back for the locket, the bank accounts here, the strange woman..." She blinked away tears. "The Hugh I knew was honest and fair-minded, but also driven and ambitious. During the war, who knows which virtues guided him. Obviously not very good ones if he never told me about all this."

At a loss, she set aside the portraits and peered into the box again. A brown envelope remained, tied with a string. Steeling herself against any more shocks, she untied it and dumped out the contents. An array of newspaper articles spilled onto the table. She rifled through them. Robert waited a moment then did the same. All the articles had to do with either the formation of Credit Mobilier—a private group organized to fund the Union Pacific Railroad—the activities of various businessmen associated with the fund, and the movements of politicians: Schuyler Colfax—Grant's former Vice President—Congressman Oakes Ames, and scores of other political figures. But all of the clippings were from the '60s.

Robert flipped the lid back over and swiped his finger along the edge, leaving a streak in the thin dust. "I don't think anyone has touched this box in years. None of these articles are more recent than 1864."

Juliet agreed, staring at an 1862 newspaper clipping from The New York Herald. It detailed the formation of the fund, which, as it happened, would turn out to be a mere cover for corruption. The Credit Mobilier scandal had not broken until '72, she recalled. Far removed from affecting her life in St. Joseph, she hadn't paid much attention to a bunch of fat-cat politicians and crooked businessmen bilking the government out of millions to benefit railroad stockholders.

Good Lord, had Hugh been involved? Had he been black-mailing someone? Had he hidden this information to keep it safe? Or *someone* safe? Safe from whom? She looked up at Robert, puzzled to see a dark scowl on his face. "What is it?"

He took a deep breath, shook his head. "I don't know. Of all the things I thought we might find here, anything to do with the railroad scandal wouldn't have even made the list. That's mostly over and done with."

Beyond frustrated, Juliet took one last look in the box. A

small square of paper remained. She picked it up and unfolded it. "FLGDB8026. What do you suppose that is?"

"A file number." Startled, they turned at the sound of Mr. Fenton's voice. He cleared his throat and nervously smoothed his tie. "That's a special designation. Land grants."

Chapter Fourteen

Settled across from Mr. Fenton in his office, Robert thought if his mind was reeling, how much more of a spin must Juliet be in. He had expected to find some evidence of wrongdoing. Selling of intelligence, protecting a Confederate spy, something showing illegal activities during the war. Hugh/Maxwell had most definitely left behind a sparse trail, but one littered with questionable, intriguing connections.

This interest in Credit Mobilier and the players in the scandal put a stunning new light on things. Perhaps Robert's focus—Army intelligence's focus—had been too narrow.

Mr. Fenton slid a piece of paper across his desk to Juliet, pulling Robert away from his cogitations. He saw the words *Land Grant* printed across the top. "That is a deed," the banker tapped the words. "A homestead. One hundred and sixty acres in Colorado."

"A homestead?" Juliet couldn't even finish. The revelations just from this bank threatened to drown her. Why had Hugh hidden *this* from her? Did the other woman live there?

Oh, Hugh! She wanted to growl and slam her fists down on the banker's desk.

"We had all of our Colorado deeds surveyed again in the

last year, a legal necessity, what with the state so recently entering the union. I can tell you that this grant is in the vicinity of a few small settlements, Animas Forks, Ouray, and a boomtown called Defiance. Other than that, it is, I gather, a remote parcel."

Juliet read the date of the grant. "He filed for this in '65." She went back to the year. She and Hugh had just met and were courting but wouldn't marry until the fall of the year. "I remember he made a trip to Austin that summer and was gone for two weeks. He said he met with investors and politicians." But now she realized, of course, he could have easily gone to Colorado. "I never questioned it." Now she questioned everything.

Robert leaned forward to get Mr. Fenton's attention. "Why do you even have the deed? Is there a lien against it?"

"No. None that we can find."

"So why is it here?" Juliet asked, her head beginning to pound.

"This is a certified copy. We were keeping it in our vault, apparently at your husband's request. A common practice. Often, the original goes with the landowner."

"Which would be where?" Robert asked softly.

"The only thing I can tell you is it's not here."

Juliet tapped her fingers on the document. "He hid this land from me. Along with a wife, a questionable military career, and who knows what else?"

Chapter Fifteen

Nashville had become quite a modern, bustling city since Robert had been here last. Reconstruction was, for the most part, complete. He didn't see any signs of the Union occupation. Nashville, re-bricked and re-painted, shone like a beacon on a hill, but moved at a pace more reminiscent of New York than a genteel, Southern city. A horse-drawn trolley rolled by, and a policeman in the intersection bade him and Juliet stop to let it pass. Across the way, a young boy in knickers tugged a girl's piggy tail and raced off down the sidewalk. Robert smiled at the mischief.

The warm summer day made the grassy-sweet smell of horse manure more pronounced, but it did not distract from the city's charms. Or his mood. He lifted his hat, shook his hair to dry the sweat trying to form on his forehead, and dropped it back in place. The policeman waved them on and Robert lightly rested his hand on Juliet's elbow to guide her. A normal, gentlemanly action, one he had done a thousand times —but not with *her*, and his mood soared higher.

Juliet Watts. After all these years, Juliet Watts marched beside him. She was alive and well, and at the tips of his fingers. The icing on the cake was this trail of conflicting, intriguing clues Hugh had left his wife. Robert loved a good mystery. He could turn over and ruminate on all these clues for hours.

A quick, sideways glance brought Robert up short. Juliet was not sharing his good mood, and he was immediately sorry for his selfishness. Face pinched, stare blank, she walked as if in a daze. She had every right to be overwhelmed, and he felt like a selfish oaf. What had they stumbled into? He wished more than anything he could be open with her about his assignment, but not yet. Not until he had a better idea of just what was going on here.

At least the key in the locket had garnered for Juliet the small amount of cash in Hugh's account—seven hundred dollars—and perhaps a far more valuable asset—the land. Fortunately, the strange woman hadn't been able to connive the bank out of the Watts estate.

He doubted she was Hugh's wife. There was no record of a woman in his life until Juliet. Though the file on his case did make reference to an unnamed female who had been on the train. What if she and the mysterious passenger Hugh's men were guarding had remained in contact after all these years? Somehow they had gotten wind that the Army was still investigating William Maxwell, A.K.A. Hugh Watts. More specifically, had found his wife.

Somehow?

Robert stopped walking. *Somehow? A leak is how.*

"What's the matter?"

And, this woman knew Hugh had accounts here and tried to beat Juliet to them. But HOW did she know? In his last telegram, all he had said was that he was following a lead to a bank in Nashville. He didn't even say which one. The woman could have guessed, he supposed, or been to all the banks in town.

But who is she?

He switched the leather satchel from beneath his right arm to his left. They'd made sure to leave the bank with everything in the safe deposit box. "After your husband died, you never heard from any of his war comrades? Or the government, or anyone who knew him in the years before he met you?"

"No one. I told you that."

"Were you ever robbed or accosted?"

"Before the other night, no." She turned to him, resting her hands on her hips. "Before you showed up at my door, my life was peaceful and quiet."

"You still want to blame me...or that locket?"

"*You* brought it to me. *I* didn't tell anyone about it."

He sighed heavily, dropping his gaze to the ground. He did look guilty as sin. But his superiors knew about Juliet. And he'd told them about the locket. "No one has ever attempted to rob you before the other night. Ever?"

"Ever. The saloon has never even been broken into."

Scratching his head, he wandered over to a bench in front of a millinery and sat down. A mole put them in a decidedly perilous position because he had no idea whom he could trust. He drummed his fingers on his thighs, thinking, reasoning. Pondering motives. Why had Juliet's file been kept open? To keep the search for her active. Why? Ostensibly, her husband had been a traitor. Did it make sense that this was a search for justice? That if Juliet were guilty of conspiracy, she would go to jail, and then this case would close?

No. Hugh/Maxwell knew something or possessed something. Information?

Robert had to assume someone either thought Juliet was the holder of that information or had access to it. Robert would bet access. The key in the locket. Which led to clues indicating Hugh had been out West at some point during the war, or immediately after.

Which led to questions about the land grant. Was there something to learn from it? Was there something hidden on it? Colorado should be Juliet's next destination, but he had to let her make that decision. He trusted she would. And he would have to send a telegram—a carefully worded telegram.

"I have to send a telegram."

Her sudden announcement, mirroring his own thoughts, startled him. "All right, we need to find the Western Union. I believe it's on Front Street."

"No." She raised her hand in front of her. "I haven't told anyone about this locket. Or the key. Or that I was coming to the bank here in Nashville. Yet, only hours before I arrive, another woman is trying to get Hugh's accounts? I know that's not a coincidence, Robert. I don't know what you're not telling me, but I know you're lying about something. None of this started until you showed up."

Her accusation delivered a stinging cut. He wanted to tell her everything, yet he could tell her nothing. In fact, at this moment, he wasn't sure whom he could tell anything. Slowly, he stood. "I don't know who that woman was." The statement was weak and a deflection.

"Maybe. Maybe not. It doesn't matter. Only the truth matters."

"If you could just trust me—"

"That's the last thing I can do. Hugh and I were barely married two years, but it feels like every minute of it was a lie. I don't have room for any more. I do have to get to the bottom of this. And it's not your journey. Unless you can tell me something to change my mind."

"Juliet—" He stopped himself. He wasn't at liberty...there was too much...she wasn't cleared...

Their gazes held. Robert prayed she would somehow see him and not the tangle of lies between them. After a moment, she shook her head. "Goodbye, Robert, and thank you."

Chapter Sixteen

Heartsick, but determined to be a man about it, Robert watched Juliet disappear into the bustling foot traffic of the Elliston Street sidewalk. He had no idea what he was going to do to stay with her, but he prayed the Lord would make a way. And He did. Of a sort.

Robert trailed behind Juliet by a good fifty yards, not fearful of losing her. After all, he knew where she was going. The same place he needed to go. A few blocks later, he hurried up beside her and opened the door to the Western Union. Her eyes widened with shock, then her brow dipped a little with annoyance, but he would have sworn he saw a touch of amusement there as well.

"I have to send a telegram, too," he fought a thin smile that would make the statement seem a lie. "I have business partners who should know my schedule."

"Ah, well," she said as they stepped inside the little office, "do you mind if I go first?"

"Certainly not."

He stood back a respectable distance while she discussed the brief note to Sam, her bartender. She would be gone longer than expected and would contact him again in a few days. Her note completed, she paid the clerk, offered him a parting smile, then headed for the door. She paused as she passed Robert. "Thank you again for all you've done for me."

He nodded but quickly stepped up to the clerk. He needed to send the telegram, but he couldn't risk losing Juliet. She might not go straight back to the hotel. He dashed off a note about the trip to the Nashville bank, providing only vague information, and that he was following up on other possibilities.

But then an idea struck him. "No, I want to redo that," he said to the clerk.

"All righty." The man picked up his pencil and stared at what he had just written, waiting for Robert. "What do you want to keep?"

"None of it."

Unfazed, the man crumpled the paper and tossed it into the waste basket. He pulled the notepad with the Western Union logo back in front of him, pencil poised to write. "Ready?"

Robert nodded. "Evidence from bank needs further examination. Will report when I have finished investigation." One last piece of bait. "Staying at Hotel Belmont."

Done, he raced back out to the street and skidded to a stop, searching left and then right for a hint of Juliet's glimmering golden hair. Not spying her, he headed for the hotel, hoping she would be there. He wished he had his journal, the book in which he wrote down thoughts, clues, and theories for cases. Often, writing things down helped him see connections, rationales, the how and why.

This case, however, left him flailing. And he ached for Juliet. One moment, she had hope her husband was not a greedy scoundrel, the next, she wasn't even sure she'd been the man's only wife. And she was right to blame Robert, or at least mistrust him. He'd brought all this to her doorstep.

He was fully aware that Juliet would not be able to think

about anything else—anyone else—until the mysteries surrounding her husband were solved. And he couldn't help her do that if she wouldn't let him on the same train with her.

He groaned out loud and ran his hands through his hair. How could he do his job if he couldn't think like anything but a lovesick teenager? He stopped at an intersection and waited for a freight wagon to roll by. He smiled at the young lady beside him, but didn't see her. Instead, the sudden confidence he was being watched whipped his head around to his left. Across the way, a small, tidy park had sprung up in Nashville, surrounded by neat, narrow brick houses. A few young mothers and their children strolled and played beneath the shady trees.

He saw no obvious spy, but knew better than to ignore this feeling. If he *was* being watched, perhaps the shadowy observer could play into his hands.

———

Juliet did not mind eating alone. The Hotel Belmont had two restaurants, a nice one and a fair-to-middling one. She decided to treat herself to the nicer one. A maître d' led her briskly through the room of white tablecloths covered with scrumptious gourmet meals. Clinking silverware and the gay laughter of women glittering with diamonds rose above the deep rumble of men speaking in amicable tones.

Her simple cotton dress was plain but clean, and she didn't give a whit what these people thought about her anyway. She wanted to eat in peace and think. Thinking in her room hadn't accomplished anything other than dragging her thoughts back to Robert. Repeatedly.

But she had to go on without him. Or so she had originally convinced herself in a fit of depression and anger over the revelations from the bank. Now, sitting here by herself, feeling the loss of his presence in a room full of people, she was second-guessing herself. Perhaps she would be better off to keep him close, to keep an eye on him, as it were.

"Juliet..."

Speak of the devil. "Robert." She looked up and reminded herself not to smile—even though the desire to fought mightily with her lips.

"I—you forgot this." He laid his leather satchel on the table. "Your papers, the clippings from the safe deposit box, the photo of Maxw—Hugh. You might need all this."

Juliet laid her hand atop it. "Thank you." She drummed her fingers for a moment, then they both spoke at once. "Robert, would you like—"

"Juliet, I need to tell—" They stopped.

She motioned to the seat opposite her. "Please sit down. Join me."

He took the seat. As she lifted her water for a sip, she noticed he subtly nudged the satchel closer to the edge of the table.

She pretended not to notice. He leaned forward. "I have to tell you some things," he said in a low, conspiratorial tone. "Things I don't think you'll want to hear."

The glass paused at her lips. The truth at any cost, she told herself, and set the water down. "Maybe, but it's time I heard them."

A waiter was passing by carrying a tray heavily loaded with meals. He raised it to avoid a man popping up out of his chair. Too late. The two collided with audible *oofs* and crashed violently into Juliet's table, nearly knocking it over. Juliet squealed as a maelstrom of food and drink rained down everywhere. Dishes shattered, littering the table and floor with food. Coffee and a red sauce splashed across the pristine tablecloth. Guests in the room gasped and gawked.

Chapter Seventeen

Robert barely managed to pull back out of the way of the downpour of food. Intent on making sure Juliet was unharmed, he reacted too late to stop the man from grabbing the satchel. The thief shoved the off-balance waiter into Robert, sending them both sprawling to the ground, in the same instant, catapulting out the door, mashed potatoes dripping from the case. Robert tossed the hapless waiter out of his way, scrambled to his feet, and raced after the man. He burst through the hotel's doors out to the street, but he was gone. And so was the satchel.

Ladies and gentlemen dressed for the opera strolled by, staring at him. A carriage rolled past at a leisurely pace, the horse's footfalls echoing cheerily off the buildings. Robert scanned the moderately busy street for any sign of a disturbance, a woman squealing, anything.

The thief had vanished. Robert clenched his fingers into a tight fist. He did not know the man, but he now knew he couldn't report to his own superior. He was alone in the cold.

He hurried back inside to find a small army of waiters and waitresses cleaning up at Juliet's table, another waitress helping her clean chicken cacciatore off her dress. The manager approached, pleading Juliet's indulgence. "Good heavens, madam, I can't apologize enough for this mishap." Robert joined them, casually flicking pasta off his shoulder. The manager handed him a napkin. "Oh, please stay and have dinner on the hotel. I'll give you our finest table."

Robert shared a hopeful glance with Juliet. She brushed at her dress again and nodded. "Yes, thank you, we would appreciate that. I'm quite hungry."

———

Juliet was pleased with the new table. She'd never eaten in such style. She and Robert were seated in a private area screened in with latticework and white, billowy curtains. Two waiters took their order, another two poured their water, another came in with an ice bucket stuffed with a bottle of champagne.

"Well, maybe the ruination of my dress will be worthwhile." A waiter had laid a napkin in her lap and she was glad she could rest her hand on it, not the remnants of the marsala sauce. Water only did so much. She would have the hotel launder the garment tonight.

Robert took his napkin off the table, snapped it open, and drifted it across his lap. "We can hope."

She was not, pleased, however, with Robert, and wanted to call him on his behavior. She studied him intently between waiters. Just what was he up to? Time to find out. "Let's get down to brass tacks. The satchel. I saw you shove it to the edge of the table."

He paused, reaching for his water, but only for a moment. "You think I wanted that man to take it?"

"That's exactly what I think."

He sighed, but followed it with a little smile, and set the water down. "I did want him to take it." She felt the disappointment roll across her face and attempted to tighten her expression.

"He stole an empty satchel, Juliet. The contents are in my room. The satchel was bait."

"And just who were you trying to catch?"

"Unfortunately, my superiors."

A waiter interrupted them, delivering a bread basket. Juliet waited for him to leave, then rested her clenched hands on the table. "Did you come to tell me everything or more nothing?"

———

"I came to tell you everything I know. And what I think I know." Robert supposed the conversation he was about to have could very well result in a court-martial, but the price didn't seem too high at the moment. He was relatively sure Juliet Watts was the only person in the world he could trust. "I am still in the Army, Juliet. I'm an intelligence officer with the Bureau of Information. And I have been looking for you for almost ten years."

She didn't react at first, but then sat back, dragging delicate fingers across the crisp, white tablecloth. "I'm listening."

"In 1864, your husband was aboard a train that transported a passenger from Richmond to Charleston. The train was attacked—as you know. Your husband was blamed by the North for an explosion that cost the lives of eleven soldiers, both Union and Confederate. Allen Pinkerton had operatives watching your husband back then, ostensibly because he was a Southern sympathizer. They said they had *reason to believe* he drew those troops into a trap.

"After the event, he disappeared. His file was never closed, and parts of it are missing or redacted. The department continued to search for your husband, whose real name, by the way, is William Maxwell. We found him again only days before the Comanche raid...at which point he died and you disappeared."

Juliet tilted her head, as if resenting the word. "You make it sound intentional." Her face sagged a little. "And his real name was Maxwell? William Maxwell." She dropped her gaze to the silverware in front of her and absently picked up the gleaming fork. "So, he *was* running from something. A murder charge."

"If you believe he was a traitor. If he was a spy, what he did —setting that bomb—was espionage. Legal, if not moral. Regardless, it took me ten years to find you."

She looked up.

He cleared his throat, shifted uncomfortably. "I mean *us*. It took us ten years."

She threw the fork down and cradled her face in her hands. Pressing her fingers to her temples, she began massaging them. "Why? What do you need me for?"

She sounded exhausted, and Robert reached for her, aching to comfort her, but withdrew his hand. "When I was initially debriefed by the Pinkertons after the Indian raid, I told them I believed you didn't know anything about your husband's real identity. I thought they let it go at that. And..." He took a long, deep breath. "And I *did* look for you for ten years. But someone else found you. I don't know who exactly. Senator Desmond Wilson, who's on the Senate Intelligence Committee, asked me to see you because I had the initial contact with you. He said if, after an investigation, I still believed you were in the dark about Maxwell's covert operations, the department would close the file on you. But I'm not sure I believe that now."

Juliet closed her eyes, breathed deeply and calmly for several moments, then peered at Robert with a mix of suspicion and grief. "Let me see if I understand. Hugh—William Maxwell—went into hiding after the event on the train. We don't know why for sure. Using the name Hugh Watts, he resurfaced in a wagon train headed for Texas. He went back for the locket because the key hidden in it opened a lockbox that left us with more clues and questions than answers."

"Yes."

"But this bureau thinks I know something about him?"

"He may have given you intelligence, or, I don't know, shared some knowledge with you that he shouldn't have."

"And they're watching to see...?"

"I suppose what you do next."

Their new meal arrived and they sat patiently while the wait staff again served the chicken marsala and lasagna, poured their water, then departed.

"Was Hugh a traitor or a spy?"

Robert shook his head, moving his lips, but couldn't make any words come out. Finally, shoulders drooping, he confessed, "The file has been..." he sighed. "Tampered with is a strong way to put it. But I believe the file has been manipulated in such a way to fog Maxwell's loyalties. Which means either he was a traitor, or he was recruited for this assignment off the books. To move that mysterious passenger. Yet, why the secret safe deposit box? Why hide things from you?" He slapped the table, his temper rising. "Why the clippings on Credit Mobilier?" He'd never had such a twisting, writhing, obfuscated case. He found it maddening.

"There must be clues from the items in the safe deposit box," she said. "We have to read every one of those articles."

"Agreed. But I thought of something else. Maxwell left the locket, which led to the key, which led to the bank, which led to the land grant and the photographs."

"You think the land grant will just lead to another clue? And another?"

"Or he's been leading us to the land grant this whole time."

Her brow furrowed with a new thought. "Who is after this information? The Army? Who?"

"That is the most important question of all. There is a mole in my department. I wired that I was staying at this hotel." He jabbed the table with his index finger. "I put the satchel out there as bait."

"And you got a bite."

"Exactly. Before we left St. Joe, I wired we were going to a bank in Nashville to examine evidence, and a mysterious woman got there mere hours before us. And, of course, there was the man who broke into your room, apparently looking for the locket."

"So, it is someone in your department? And we're on our own?"

"No. At least, I hope not. I have one contact I've been thinking I'll go to directly. Senator Wilson. But I'm just not sure..."

"I want to leave, Robert. I want to go tonight. I want to see the land...and I want you to go with me...if you will."

He tapped his fingers on the table and tried not to look too pleased by the invitation. "I think you're right. I'll send another telegram, one that will throw them off our trail for at least a day or two."

Chapter Eighteen

"Senator, these came for you just a moment ago."

Senator Wilson continued with the letter he was writing, but raised his hand to take the messages from his aide. When he heard his door shut, he opened them.

The first was a note written on Bureau of Military Information letterhead.

M advised us operative retrieved the satchel, but it was empty. Hall and Watts left Nashville during the night. She has lost them, but merely temporary setback. I believe Hall suspects he cannot trust his department. M and I believe, therefore, he will contact you, and I will have operatives at your disposal. —Col. Arnett

Unhappy with this news, Senator Wilson opened the telegram.

HAVE SNEAKED OUT OF NASHVILLE. FEAR A MOLE. NEED TO PROTECT MRS. WATTS. HEADED TO DEFIANCE, COL. LAND GRANT IN HUGH WATTS'S NAME COULD BE PIVOTAL CLUE. CAN I LOOK TO YOU FOR ASSISTANCE IF NEEDED?

Well, there was hope after all. His presidential ambitions were still alive then. He pulled a fresh sheet of paper from his desk drawer, jittered the fountain pen between his fingers for a moment, then penned his response, a half-smile creeping across his lips.

LT. HALL, TRUST ME. WHATEVER YOU NEED. HAVE NO FURTHER CONTACT WITH YOUR DEPT. KEEP ME APPRISED.

He slid the telegram off to the side and started a note.

Col. Arnett, yes, you are compromised. Hall is aware of the leak. Not my involvement, however. He telegrammed to say he and Mrs. Watts are going to Defiance, Colorado. Something to do with a land grant. He believes they may have found the final clue. I am leaving tonight for Denver—

His hand paused. Was that wise? Better to be close and able to control the flow of information, especially since he didn't know Millicent's exact whereabouts. Yes, he would go to Denver. Satisfied with this course of action, he added to the note:

Get an operative to Defiance immediately. Gather the evidence and close all doors.

After a moment's hesitation, the senator underlined *close all doors.*

Twice.

———

Juliet could not read another newspaper article on credit, bank stocks, railroad statistics, or the Civil War and its economic impact on transcontinental transportation. Rubbing her eyes, she still saw the names of the Credit Mobilier politicians and businessmen swirling in her mind. It had to be well past midnight. How long had they been traveling? A day and a half? Two? She'd lost track of the sunsets. The windows on the train were pitch black.

O so weary, she leaned her head back on the cushioned seat and yawned. The peaceful sway of the locomotive and the touch of Robert's arm sharing the armrest with her comforted

her, begged her to sleep. She pressed her hands to the newspaper clippings in her lap so they wouldn't slip away and closed
her eyes, entertaining the idea of a nap.

"I have the names of the board of directors for Credit
Mobilier going around in my head like a nursery rhyme." He
didn't reply. She sensed his gaze, though, and turned her face
to him. Her eyes still closed, she said, "Penny for your
thoughts."

After a moment, he said softly, "I'm sorry, Juliet."

His apology didn't surprise her. She knew he was referring
to the revelations about Hugh. All the lies. The secrets. The
questions. She wanted to hide in the darkness behind her lids
for a little while longer. She didn't want Robert's pity. It made
her feel weak and less than capable.

Juliet decided to tell him just that. "Your sympathy makes
me feel...foolish—no, ashamed." She was surprised at herself
for admitting such a personal truth.

"Ashamed?"

She heard him shift in the seat, felt the warmth of his
breath on her face as he apparently drew closer. Slowly, she
opened her eyes. He had rested both elbows on the armrest
and was staring intently at her, his face mere inches from hers.
Her heartbeat quickened its pace instantly.

"What do you have to be ashamed of? That's absurd."

"Maybe." She shrugged. "Most likely. But it's how I feel. It's
the shame a woman feels who's married to an alcoholic or a
wife-beater. The silent judgment that she should have known
better, or left him when things got bad."

"You had no way of knowing, Juliet. If he was a spy, he was
trained at deception."

"And if he was a traitor?"

"Then he was born with the ability to deceive."

Comforted some by his compassion, she let her gaze drift
away from his eyes, so warm and sincere, down his nose, to his

mouth. His jaw had darkened with beard stubble, but she liked it.

His lips twitched into a slight smile. "I gave up on you twice. Or tried to and, yet, here we are."

"Gave up?"

He took a long, deep breath and pursed his lips as if determining to follow through on something. "It *was* me. I looked for you for ten years, Juliet. You're the reason I transferred into the Bureau of Military Information."

She blinked, pulled back a touch. What was he saying? "Did you think me guilty? That I was a part of Hugh's web of deceit?"

He snorted softly. "Hardly."

"Then why look for me?" And why did her heart start racing, her breath come shorter and shorter, when he drew close like this? Why did she want so badly for Robert Hall to kiss her?

He pinched a little sweat off his lip. "You're not going to make this easy, are you?"

"I don't know."

He chuckled. Nodded. "I—I—" A quizzical frown creased his brow. "How is it that you are not married again, Mrs. Watts?"

Juliet inclined her head, baffled by this conversation, by his sudden change of direction. "Simply put...it's easier being alone."

"You mean you're afraid of getting hurt? All these years, you've just hidden yourself away because it's safer?"

"Oh, that sounds like some drivel an English romance writer would spout." She tore her gaze from him with a disgusted sigh and stared at the lamp overhead. "I simply mean I do well alone. I run my business. I work hard. I stay busy. I don't get lonely." She shrugged a shoulder. "Love is for young, rosy-cheeked maidens. Who haven't been jaded by the world."

"You haven't forgiven him." He sounded confident, as if

he'd made a brilliant deduction, striking upon the crux of the matter. "You've encased your heart in brick. You won't forgive him. You won't fall in love. You won't get hurt again."

Hugh. No. She hadn't forgiven him. Or God. And Robert Hall was annoyingly...insightful. "I don't like having...my *heart* examined as if it were a frog in a medical class."

"Am I wrong?"

Now she *didn't* want to look at him, but couldn't seem to stop herself. Was that hope glimmering in his eyes? "Why did you search for me?"

The moment hung between them. His mouth moved, but he uttered no words. He scratched his nose and grinned sheepishly. "I was eighteen, Juliet, when we found you... I—I don't know how to explain it. I just...you just...you wouldn't...leave my mind."

She almost had pity on him. He sounded as if the words were being dragged from him by a team of wild horses. The confession, whatever it regarded, weighed on him and perplexed her.

"Those last words of yours. That you *did* mind if I prayed for you." Exhaling what sounded like exasperation, he turned away, settled back again. "I'm making no sense. I can't..." he faded off, but added with finality, "I can't."

Juliet realized her mouth was agape and snapped it shut. What was this poor man trying to tell her? Unexpected disappointment grappled with confusion. She attempted to help him. "You've worried about my *soul* for a decade?"

He hissed derisively through his teeth. "I have made a royal mess of this." He groaned and ran his hand through his hair, then rubbed the back of his head. "I've fought Indians, chased bank robbers, ridden in posses after murderers, and yet I can't..." He licked his lips and stared at the floor, an expression of utter disgust on his face. "I am a complete coward."

"Robert, I have no idea what...?" She circled her hand in the air, clueless. And she certainly wouldn't dare hope...

"And that right there tells me you have no idea...nothing I've said...you have no inkling—" He bit that off, and rose to his feet. "I'm going to stretch my legs. Excuse me."

"Robert, if you want to talk to me about...God or...I'll be polite and listen."

He grimaced. She had the definite feeling that somehow the suggestion had made things worse. He sliced the air, cutting off the suggestion. "Eventually, maybe." He said nothing else, hesitated for a moment, then marched past her, down the aisle, and out of the car.

Baffled, Juliet absently patted the newspaper clippings into a neater stack and slipped them back into the new satchel. She had no idea what to make of Robert's...blathering.

He'd looked for her for ten years?

It would be ridiculous to think he'd done so for reasons of the heart. As he'd said, he'd only been eighteen. Perhaps he felt as if he'd failed in sharing the gospel with her. That because she didn't want him to pray with her somehow reflected on him, his witness? The possibility left her...

Be honest, Juliet. A little disappointed.

She sat quietly for a while, fingers drumming on the satchel. When he came back, she'd get the man to just spit it out. Whatever *it* was. To speak plain and let the truth fall where it may. She wanted to know what was on his mind. She'd had enough of hidden truths. She wanted her questions—and her *hope*—settled. Firmly.

After half an hour, though, he still hadn't returned. Fine. She made up her mind to find him and pull the truth from him, if she had to use a block and tackle.

Chapter Nineteen

Robert hunched his shoulders against the chill on the observation platform, exhaled the smoke from his cigarette, but he still wasn't ready to go back inside. He had dealt with the fact that Juliet not only didn't seem to give a whit about him, she'd resigned herself to widowhood for the rest of her life. Disgusted, he tossed the smoke over the rail and wished he hadn't left his hat inside. His head was cold.

Gazing out over the moon-washed plains and towering Kansas corn, Robert couldn't understand why he was here. *With you, God, all things are possible. I suppose you can change her mind, but otherwise, I've spent ten years just going in circles.*

He thought of the women he'd walked away from because he'd been so certain he wasn't called to marry either of them. Now, he doubted his hearing. "Maybe I misunderstood. Maybe I've heard wrong all along, Lord."

Frustrated, he slapped the rail. "Well, I'm done. I've hunted her down, daydreamed about her, hung my heart on my sleeve for nearly a decade, over nothing more than a memory. I must be crazy." He stared up at the moon, trying to keep from raising his fist to heaven. "If I haven't wasted all these years, Lord, give me some encouragement. Or let me go home."

"Robert?"

He flinched and grasped the rail, but didn't turn around.

"Who are you talking to?" She gasped. "I'm sorry. You were praying."

He chuckled, but it was bitter. "Yes, I was." He expected her to leave. When she didn't, he did turn around.

Arms crossed, she was tapping her foot. "I'm sorry for the interruption. But *we* have to talk."

Hope flared in him. She'd sought him out. *Encouragement?* "All right."

She drifted over to the rail, clutched it for a moment, then faced him. "Just say it. Whatever you were trying to tell me. I'll deal with it. You think I'm a spy. You think I'm hiding something. You didn't thump your Bible in my face. Whatever is bothering you—has been bothering you for ten years—just toss it out on the table. See where the chips fall."

Moonlight shimmered in her golden tresses, sparkled in her eyes like diamonds. It played invitingly on the curves of her cheeks and the hollow of her throat as she gazed up at him with her jaw set. What was it about her that stirred a longing deep within him, like the feeling of a weary soul meeting its long-sought destiny? The way he felt about her made no sense at all.

How could she be so blind and not see his heart?

The back of the train was breezy and the air lifted a strand of her hair across her face. In a move as natural to him as breathing, Robert swept it off, back behind her ear, and his hand froze.

Juliet's eyes widened, but she didn't move.

She didn't move.

Strangely certain he was walking a tight wire, he drifted his thumb over her cheekbone. Her breathing hitched, then sped up, her chest rising and falling faster.

Even as he lowered his lips to hers, the thought crossed his mind, *this might ruin everything,* but he couldn't stop himself. The desire—the *need*—to hold her overwhelmed his fears. This moment begged for a kiss, a kiss that he'd wanted for ten years. Their lips met, stiff, a little questioning at first, but then a dam burst. Heat, white-hot and searing, coursed through him as she parted her lips and she tilted up to him.

Yielding.

He pulled her into a crushing embrace, encircling her waist, molding himself against her every curve, every line. She laid her hands on his shoulders, clutched his shirt—*clinging,* he thought, *not pushing me away.* He deepened the kiss, desperate for her, starved for her. She responded with her own hunger that set his senses on fire, made his hands ache to touch, caress...know that she was real.

She jerked back with a gasp, eyes wide with terror. He tried not to let her go, but she stepped out of his embrace, her chest heaving. His hands went cold from the emptiness.

At first, she merely gawked in terror. Finally, she whispered, "I didn't come out here for that."

While that didn't ring quite true to Robert, based on her terrified expression, he wasn't sure what to say. He couldn't think anyway, so fogged was his brain from the kiss. Slowly, he lowered his hands, a realization dawning on him. She was as skittish as a new foal. For all that tough talk, Juliet Watts was scared to death of her feelings. Or *feeling,* in general.

"Well, I won't lie, I'm a little disappointed to hear that." His honesty only prompted a confused pinch in her brow. Puzzled, he ran his fingers through his hair. What could he say that might put her at ease? "And if it never happens again..." He tried to force the heat from his face, "I have to say it was well worth the wait."

"You were waiting for me out here?"

"No." He chuckled. "No. For the first time in a decade, I wasn't." Didn't that beat all. He'd given up...and here she was.

Though, by the looks of her—those wild eyes and clenched hands—she was on the verge of leaping from the train. Still, he would definitely call what had just transpired *encouraging*. He had to handle her carefully, though. Move slow. Earn her trust. "Umm, why don't we go back inside. You're shivering."

Her mouth moved, soundlessly. She nodded, then abruptly shook her head. "No. Games like that won't work on me, Mr. Hall. I won't be distracted. I still want—I want to know what you were trying to tell me."

Games? She can't be this thickheaded. Robert dropped his hands on his hips, studied the platform's floor for a moment. She doesn't *want* to see. She's too scared to see. You can lead a horse to water...

But how do you convince her there aren't any alligators in the pond?

Maybe you just have to make her thirsty enough. "Juliet, I will tell you. I promise." He looked up. "But I can't right now." Before she could argue, he side-stepped to the door and opened it for her. "And just so you know, I don't play those sorts of games, Mrs. Watts."

———

Juliet's body sang, her legs wobbled, threatened to buckle as she walked back to her seat. Only now was her heart coming back to something akin to a normal pace. How long since she'd felt passion like that? She sneaked a quick glance at him. Did he care about her...could it be possible? The idea terrified her.

She reached their seats and nearly collapsed into hers. A moment later, he settled beside her. Seeming to have a second thought, he rose high enough to reach the lamp over their heads and dimmed it.

"I'm going to try to get a little rest. The conductor said we won't be in Colorado Springs till morning." He turned his back to Juliet and leaned his head on the cushion.

She nearly gasped. He could just go to sleep? Leave her like this...

Like what, Juliet? Like what?

Like she wanted more.

The confession stunned her.

Chapter Twenty

In Colorado Springs, they learned they would need to take the stage to Defiance. A short ride. Four or five hours. Perhaps if Hugh's homestead wasn't too far, they could be there tonight. Juliet waffled between excitement and something she couldn't name. Fear of the unknown? Dread of a dramatic change?

The stage was crowded—eight passengers, in all. She traveled nearly four hours with Robert pressed against her. His face inches from hers when they talked. She had to concentrate to keep her eyes trained on his and not let them roam over his face, now arguably sporting a full beard. She didn't mind. It added character.

The stage road rose rapidly in elevation, and when a strong, cool breeze hit her, Juliet took a gander out the window. She gasped. The sheer cliff beside them, a thousand feet of sheer rock punctuated here and there with cedars and sage, made her stomach do a stunned roll. Every bounce and jostle in the road after that had her clutching Robert's arm.

"I should never have looked out the window."

As if challenged, he leaned across her, glanced out the window, then pulled back, holding her gaze. "No recovering from that fall."

His words seemed to have added meaning, but she couldn't think. His eyes, his lips, held a fascination for her now. One that frightened her more than the cliff outside the stagecoach. Frightened her, yet, drew her like a moth to a flame.

And look how that works out for the moth, she reminded herself.

He seemed to linger an instant longer than necessary, then settled back again. A particularly jarring bump in the road worked a squeak from her and a few of the other ladies. Robert embraced her, just instinctive, she assumed, and she didn't protest.

Maddeningly, he waited a moment, then said, "My apologies. A woman squeals and it seems to come naturally to hold her." His gaze drifted to her mouth. "I should let go."

No, no, no. His arm felt so warm and safe and comforting.

"You two ain't married, you oughta consider it." The old man sitting across from them winked at Robert. "Or run the other way, son, if you still can." The other passengers chuckled merrily at the joke.

The corner of Robert's mouth ticked up. "Oh, I can still run." As if to prove it, he released Juliet and leaned back against the leather.

Run? From her? Was he merely joking with the old man? Then their kiss had been a mere dalliance? Wasn't that what she wanted it to be? Why couldn't she make sense of any of this?

Overwhelmed by the questions, a touch rejected, she pressed against the seat, too, but stared out the window. Mid-afternoon sun streamed through a thin forest of pines as the stage rocked and bumped its way toward Defiance. So, he could still run. Well *of course* he could. He needed to be able to move on when this was all over.

That would be best for them both.

She couldn't deny, though, how empty the thought left her.

———

Juliet slipped past Robert as he held the door open into what served in Defiance for the city hall—a former saloon. A saloon that was obviously closed. The shelves were empty of liquor. The green-topped tables were devoid of cards and chips. Not to mention, there were no customers. The place was a graveyard.

"This is *not* how I imagined the legendary Iron Horse Saloon," Robert said, twirling his hat in his hands.

"Because it's closed." A voice, thick with a velvety Southern accent, floated down from above them. They followed the sound to a man standing at the top of the stairs.

Running a saloon, Juliet had seen a lot of handsome men, but Charles McIntyre was just this side of stunning. Dark, wavy hair curled over his collar and shimmered like coal as he descended the stairs. Piercing blue eyes, a devastating smile, and the most perfectly trimmed, narrow beard she'd ever seen made his face unforgettable. He plucked a pocket watch from his red silk vest and checked the time. "I was just on my way out, but if I can be of service—"

"Do you know the name William Maxwell?" Juliet did not miss the slight hitch in the man's step. Encouraged, she pressed further. "Or perhaps Hugh Watts?"

Mr. McIntyre's face darkened, caution putting an edge on those handsome features. "What's this about?"

Robert stepped forward and offered his hand. "Forgive us. It's been an interesting journey getting here. I'm Robert Hall, Lieutenant Robert Hall." They shook hands. "And this is Juliet Watts, the wife—widow—of Hugh Watts. You may have known him as William Maxwell."

Mr. McIntyre's face lit up as he shook Juliet's hand, but almost as quickly dimmed with sadness. "I am sorry to hear Hugh is no longer with us. I had hoped he would return to Defiance one day."

"So you knew him?" She had to fight to keep her voice even, excitement tugging at her as it was. "And he's been here? As Watts or Maxwell?"

"Ostensibly, Hugh Watts." His answer puzzled her—Robert, too, she judged by his stiffened countenance. Mr. McIntyre smiled. "You must be Juliet. He wrote his brother about you. I can see now why he did not rush back to Colorado."

"Mr. McIntyre, I'm trying to find out just who my husband was. Perhaps you can help me. I certainly have more questions than answers."

He shoved a hand into his pocket and regarded her thoughtfully. "I suppose you do. Let me get us some coffee and we'll compare notes."

———

"How long has Hugh been gone?" Mr. McIntyre asked as he poured coffee for the group seated at one of his poker tables.

"Nearly ten years."

His eyes widened. "Ten?" His distant expression said his mind was racing as he finished pouring and sat down. "I suspected as much, but that long? What in the world brings you here now?"

"I seemed to have stumbled onto some puzzling questions about my husband. Please tell me how you knew him."

"Hugh and I met in Texas at the end of the war. He had left the South and was not returning. I shared that ambition, as did a few of my compatriots.

"On the rumor of gold, we eagerly made our way here to Colorado—well, Hugh was perhaps not as eager as we. He was thinking of settling in Rimfire. You don't know any of this?"

Juliet shook her head. "He rarely talked about anything prior to meeting me on the wagon train to Texas."

This seemed to mystify Mr. McIntyre. "Well, in any event,

he changed his mind and came with us. Hugh's brother James—"

"Brother?" Juliet wondered how many more family members were going to come slithering out of the woodpile. A wife—real or not—and now a brother? "He said his brother was dead."

Mr. McIntyre shook his head. "Not in '65. James joined up with us in Denver and we proceeded on here to the San Juan Valley.

"Hugh, James, and two other members in the party decided to separate and scout further south, down the San Miguel River. The rest of us continued north. A fateful decision." He paused for several seconds here, his gaze frosting over. "One could argue Watts made the wiser choice. My party fell under attack by Utes. Nearly killed us all.

"Watts, on the other hand, found some land he liked and said he was going to claim it under the Homestead Act.

"Which, to my understanding, he did, and he left his brother on it to fulfill the legal requirements—construction of a permanent dwelling, various other improvements as required by law—so that he could return to Texas."

So far, Juliet followed this tale. She had met Hugh on the wagon train headed to Texas, they had both decided to stay in Rimfire. Not long after their arrival, he had disappeared for a few weeks, maybe a month, but upon his return had ardently courted her. She'd never thought much about his absence— only that he had returned with a simple explanation of having attended to some business.

"Hugh said he would be back within a year, but in the meantime, James had full charge of the homestead. To do with as he saw fit.

"Now I come to the part that will interest you. I overheard Hugh and James talking. Hugh was going to claim the home-stead under a *nom de plume*. Hugh Watts was the *false* name. His real name was William Maxwell. Further, without explanation, he directed James not to reveal their true identities to anyone. Just lay low and build the ranch up in Hugh's absence, as he needed to settle some unfinished business. We suspected it had something to do with his wartime activities. James believed his brother had been a spy—though he was not sure for which side—and that had caused some hard feelings."

"I find it interesting," Robert interrupted, "that you are privy to so much information."

The subtle suspicion seemed to annoy Mr. McIntyre. "I am a man who can keep a confidence, Mr. Hall. James recognized that right off and he needed loans to get the ranch up and running. He told me the truth so I would know what I was getting into. Otherwise, he wouldn't have ever seen a penny. I'm only telling you because I recognize Juliet from a picture."

The explanation seemed to satisfy Robert and he nodded slightly.

Brushing off the distraction, Mr. McIntyre continued. "A few months after *William* left, he wrote James and said he would be delayed in returning to Colorado by perhaps as much as a year or more, as he was getting married.

"And that was the last communication James received from William. Almost ten years now." He nodded, confirming Juliet's dates. "We naturally assumed that Maxwell had stopped communicating because either he didn't want to or wasn't able to. It didn't make sense that he would walk away from the homestead, so we were inclined to believe the latter.

"Your arrival heralds both joy and pain. I am sorry to hear Hugh is no longer with us, as I said, but I can see why he returned to Texas. What happened, if I may ask?"

"We were caught in a Comanche raid. I survived. Hugh didn't."

"I see. And, forgive me, Lieutenant Hall. How are you involved in this matter?"

It took Robert several seconds to answer. Juliet wondered how much he would tell. "I returned a locket to Mrs. Watts that I came into possession of as a result of that Indian raid. We discovered it held a key that led to a bank, where we found out about this land grant."

"Then, as the widow, you've come to take possession of the ranch, Mrs. Watts?"

"No—No, I uh..." The thought hadn't even crossed her mind. Too many other ideas and questions whirled in her mind. "I just want to know if my husband is a traitor or a spy. He died saving that locket. But he never breathed a word to me about living under a false name, that his brother was still alive, that he owned a homestead, much less that he had another wife."

Mr. McIntyre's brow rose. "A wife besides you?"

"A young lady beat us to the bank by mere hours the other day," Robert explained. "She was trying to get into Watts's safe deposit box."

"He never mentioned a family, or a wife, but that doesn't mean he didn't have one, I suppose."

Juliet remembered the satchel and rifled through it quickly, pulling out the photo. "Among the items in the box, we found this."

She passed it to Mr. McIntyre, who studied it carefully. "Hugh. And that's James, his brother." He pointed at the man in the background standing near the tent. "And that is Maurice Perlot. He returned east." He studied the photo for another second. "This photo was taken on the homestead."

Chapter Twenty-One

Mr. McIntyre returned the photo and leaned back in his chair. "So, we have a man who may or may not have a dark past fleeing the South immediately after the war. He claims land in Colorado, hides it from his bride, along with his real identity, and settles with her in Texas. No wonder you have questions, Mrs. Watts. But you still puzzle me, Mr. Hall. Your involvement in all this."

Robert suspected very little got by Mr. McIntyre, but that didn't mean he had to make getting the details easy. "The mystery fascinates me, and Mrs. Watts needed an escort. She was going to track down these clues on her own. I didn't think that was safe."

"Uh, huh." Mr. McIntyre crossed one leg over the other. Clearly, he didn't believe a word from Robert's mouth. He could only assume, however, that the man had no way of figuring out his ties to military intelligence. "Yes, it is a mystery. In my experience, there are really only two reasons a man will hide his past. To protect himself...or someone he loves."

"Which do you think it is?" Juliet asked.

"I have no idea. Hugh never confided in me. I will say this.

James has invested quite a bit of time, energy, and money in that ranch. He thinks of it as his. I'm not sure how pleased he'll be to discover his brother left a widow—one with legal claims to his property. I would suggest caution."

This seemed to signal the end of how Mr. McIntyre could help them. Juliet rose and the men followed. "I thank you for the information." She shook Mr. McIntyre's hand with a pained expression. "I don't think it's helped, unfortunately."

"Maybe not yet." Robert reached out to shake Mr. McIntyre's hand as well. He knew from past cases, sometimes information drizzled down like the chaos of confetti, and then suddenly all the pieces formed a picture. "We keep gathering pieces, a picture will present itself. Something you told us here today may help everything fall into place."

"Perhaps." Mr. McIntyre followed them to the door and opened it. "James's place is about a four-hour ride. The livery is at the end of town. Don't dally and you'll get there before dark." With a nod, he let Juliet pass by, but stopped Robert with a hand to his shoulder. "I said James is dangerous. He's fast with the ladies. He sees her as a threat, he may try to sweep her off her feet. And I suspect you'll resent that."

On the busy street, a balking, unruly mule and a group of miners passing by mercifully drowned out Robert's awkward response. Charles McIntyre, the once-famous brothel-owner and unquestioned authority in Defiance, offered a wry smile as he removed his hand. Still formidable, Robert guessed, the man was more *human* than he had expected.

Stepping out, he had to hold the door for the *cause* of that humanity, and he couldn't help but stare. A pretty, petite blonde wearing a tailored sky-blue dress and a long, golden braid acknowledged him with a polite nod and then slipped into McIntyre's arms.

And the man *melted*.

Every hard, dangerous edge on this legendary lawless rogue disappeared. Robert grinned. McIntyre grinned back over the lovely lady's head. A little bit awed, Robert quietly closed the door.

Wishing Juliet had seen the interaction, he was surprised to discover her staring at the entrance. Her cheeks were flushed, and he wondered if there was any chance she was replaying their kiss on the train, longing for a love that would melt Robert like that.

Did she long for a drink of water, a taste of him, yet? Enough to face the imaginary danger in the water? Would she ever be that desperate, that thirsty?

Wishing he could ask, he denied the urge with great effort and dropped his hat in place. He let two miners in mud-encrusted plaid amble by—each of them appreciatively tipping their hats to Juliet—then crossed over to her. "Let's go find that livery."

————

As Juliet and Robert ambled down the busy boardwalk, she noted their slow pace and wondered if they were thinking about the same thing.

"Funny thing to see a man with his reputation humbled by love."

His comment answered her question. "The boys back at my saloon would say castrated by it." Juliet immediately regretted the observation, especially when she saw the way Robert stiffened and his jaw tensed.

"What do you say?"

She hated these introspective questions of his. "I don't know." She shrugged a shoulder dismissively. "Love isn't anything I'm an expert on. Clearly."

"You think it makes a man weak or strong to love like that?"

"Like what?"

He thought for a moment. "Unwaveringly." He raised a

finger. "And don't try to change the subject."

She took a deep breath, ruing this conversation. Love had never been anything but a lie to her. She couldn't fathom it being real. She supposed it had to be, though. People throughout history had done stunning, beautiful, sacrificial things in its name. "I suppose it's like anything you commit your heart and soul to. It has to make you stronger because..." She searched for her meaning. "Because it's something bigger than you. Than your own needs." Not everyone, in fact, obviously most people, did not find this fabled loved. But Robert—she slid her gaze over to him—he might. After all, he said he'd looked for her for ten years—

A stunning possibility stopped Juliet as if she'd walked into a wall.

"What's the matter?" Robert turned to her, his brow creased with concern. "Are you all right?"

"Umm..." She looked at him, his messy hair poking out from under his Stetson, mesmerizing blue eyes meeting hers, clothes wrinkled and dirty from their day on the stage. He needed a shave and a bath. And yet, he was...he created in her...a *yearning*. Not just for love but for the ability to surrender to it.

She shook her head, disgusted with her inability or unwillingness to mine this subject. "I don't know. I mean, no. Let's get some horses or a wagon or something."

Juliet hurried away from Robert as if little dogs were nipping at her heels.

———

The wagon topped the crest of a hill and Juliet touched Robert's arm. He understood and tugged on the reins, stopping the horse.

The ranch below—made up of a two-story log cabin, several outbuildings, and three massive corrals—nestled itself among green, grassy hills that rolled before them like a lazy day at sea. Cattle grazed everywhere, clusters of white-faced herds interrupted here and there by milling groups of horses also enjoying the summer grass. Long shadows stretched out across the panorama like lolling fingers.

All around the valley, dramatic snow-capped peaks reminded Robert they were resting in the arms of the San Juan range. "It's beautiful here." He liked the West. At least this much of it. He'd spent most of the last decade in the South and Midwest, tracking bandits through swamps and high humidity. This air and this view could spoil a man.

"Let's hope it's more than that," Juliet said. "Let's hope it's the final piece in the puzzle."

Robert could only imagine how tired she must be of the questions and the uncertainty about Hugh—whether he was a hero or a villain. Almost as eager as she to get answers, he snapped the reins and the horse trotted down the hill and into the heart of the ranch. A man exited from the barn at the sound of their approach, a bucket in his hand.

He didn't frown at their presence, merely nodded. "Can I help you?"

"We're looking for James Wa—" Juliet stumbled. "Watts. James Watts."

Robert knew right away this man was James Watts. The family resemblance wasn't as obvious in the photograph. In person, it was more pronounced. His face was wider than Hugh's, a touch less angular, but still the resemblance was there, around his deep-set, dark eyes. James's hair was dark and he wore it longer, just past his collar. And, instantly grating on Robert's nerves, he wielded a rakish smile as he subtly appraised Juliet.

He set the bucket down and took her hand in his. "Juliet. The photo I have of you is old, but I'd know you anywhere. You're even more beautiful in person."

He left her stammering, but she recovered quickly. "I see which brother got the gift of blarney."

James chuckled. "Yes, big brother got the brains." He scanned the area around them, paused only briefly on Robert. "Where is the scoundrel? I think ten years is a little long to go without writing."

Juliet covered his hands with hers. "He's not coming, James. I'm sorry. He passed away years ago."

The man took a deep breath, absorbing the news. Wincing, he exhaled it slowly. "I guess I knew. He never would have gone that long without getting in touch. But when I saw you, I hoped."

"I'm sorry."

He smiled sadly, but then acknowledged Robert with a nod, attempting to move past the awkward moment. "I'm James Watts. Are you her husband?"

"What?" Robert's eyes bugged. "No. No. I—I…"

"James," Juliet interrupted. "I didn't know about you. We need to talk. Can we go inside?"

———

James stared at the picture in the locket, lying on the kitchen table, surrounded by the newspaper clippings and the photo. Hesitantly, he picked it up. "It's been so long… We grew up in Maryland. Near the Chesapeake. Did he ever tell you that?"

Robert would have guessed no, judging by the hurt expression on Juliet's face.

"No. He said you died at Bull Run. He also *said* you were orphans and had moved from home to home. When the state turned him out at sixteen, he worked odd jobs until the war started."

James laughed, but it sounded bitter and empty. "We fished. A lot. Our father owned a fishing boat. And Will and I were close until the war. We enlisted together, but never served in the same unit. In fact, we didn't see each other for five years, till I met up with him in Denver in '65. That's when we came west looking for land."

"Yes." Robert absently picked up a newspaper clipping. "We talked to Charles McIntyre in Defiance. He filled us in on a few details."

James dropped the picture and eyed Robert with suspicion. "I'm sorry, tell me this again. You just happened to return this locket to Juliet, and that's when all the graves started opening?"

The two men locked gazes. At face value, the scenario did make Robert sound guilty, but he couldn't tell this man he was an intelligence officer. At least not yet. Not until he knew what Hugh was hiding...and what James might be after. "I was on my way to the gold fields. I heard about a woman in St. Joe who kept a corset on display in her saloon—a corset that still had the hole from an arrow in it. There couldn't be too many of those—especially with the owner still alive."

James gawked at Juliet. "I've heard that story. That's you?"

"The corset saved my life. But the locket cost Hugh his. Take the picture out."

Brow furrowed in confusion, James peeled the photo out. Juliet had replaced the key. Her brother-in-law picked it up. "This goes to the safe deposit box?" She and Robert both nodded, but James again speared Robert with a suspicious gaze. "How did you come to have it?"

"Robert pulled the arrow out of me. He saved my life."

"I tried to give her the locket in the hospital, right after the attack. She didn't want it. I hung on to it just in case I ever ran into her again."

"And you did. What are the odds that you just *ran into her*."

Juliet slid her hand over to James's but he kept his eyes on Robert. "All these years, James, I have hated Hugh because I believed he risked our lives for a paltry bauble. I think I was wrong. I think he may have had a more noble reason."

Finally, James shifted his stare from Robert to Juliet. "I doubt it."

———

James rose and went to the stove. "Can I pour either of you some coffee?" They both declined. He poured one for himself, but didn't return to the table. Instead, he stayed at the stove, staring at the burners, but he was seeing something else. "We both enlisted in the Union army. Then I heard he'd switched sides. It didn't really surprise me. William Maxwell didn't care for slavery, but he didn't ever skip out on a money-making venture. If he was fighting for the South, then there was some money to be made." He turned around and leaned on the stove, holding his coffee halfway up. "In Denver, he told me he did what he had to do. That was all. No big explanation. No speech." He sipped the coffee, Juliet thought, to hide his disappointment. "He did ask me to forgive him. He was sorry he'd disgraced the family and said someday he'd try to explain."

Juliet's own disappointment welled within her. A traitor. That was all. Hugh had switched sides because he saw an opportunity. It made sense. At least partially. She wouldn't deny that her husband had a very pragmatic, entrepreneurial side.

But this didn't explain everything. She'd come here for the end result. Surely, they had to be close. She had hoped the locket would lead to an altruistic reason for Hugh's behavior, but barring that, she just wanted to know what he had died for. "Can you think of any reason he would have laid out clues leading us here?"

Robert jumped in here. "Did he ever say or do anything that would lead you to believe he was hiding something on the land?" Juliet and James gaped at him. He shrugged. "What do you think we're looking for? Smoke?"

"No..." Juliet frowned. "Money. I thought we would find cash. Or gold. Or...I don't know...."

"I don't have any answers either, but my best guess is Hugh knows something about someone and he's hidden incriminating information somewhere either for safekeeping..." Their stares demanded he finish. "Or he was blackmailing someone."

Juliet flinched. "Back to that. He was good. He was bad. He was a saint. He was a devil."

"I'm sorry, Juliet. I'm trying to see the whole picture. I will say, Mr. McIntyre got me thinking. A man hides his past to protect himself or someone else. Now, I don't know what he did during the war, but I'm betting this false name"—he looked at James— "was to protect you." He switched his gaze to Juliet. "And then you. Whatever he did, for whatever reason, I think was trying to keep you both out of it."

"Mighty decent of him," James muttered.

Robert rose and paced the kitchen floor, rubbing his chin. "I just can't figure out what or who his information affects. And why would it matter after all this time?"

Silence fell and Juliet sensed them all digging deep, striving desperately for some insight they didn't currently have. She drummed her fingers on the table, then opened the locket and pulled out the trimmed photo of Hugh. She reached across the table and handed it to James. "Read the back. Does it mean anything to you?"

Setting his coffee down, James took the picture. "Luke 19:39-40?" He shrugged. "My Bible is a little—"

"Jesus says if they keep their peace, the rocks will cry out."

"Oh." Again, he shrugged. "Sorry. Not ringing a bell."

Robert spun. "Are there any notable rock formations on the land? Or, were there any structures here when you got the homestead?"

"There are a couple of shacks and such, and a few rocky buttes. Over the years, I've bought up several neighboring spreads. One of them has a cave. I don't think Will—*Hugh* would have known about it, though."

"Well, those buttes might be a place to start." Robert dragged his hand through his hair. "All these clues led here."

"Not all of them."

Juliet tapped the newspaper clippings. "There's something in here we're not seeing."

Robert sucked in a cheek and nodded. "You're right. He saved those for a reason. We'll go through them again tonight and see some of the rocks tomorrow." He sat down opposite her. "I still think we're almost at the end of this. Almost."

She'd have her answers. And Robert would have—

James dropped his tin cup on the stove, the sound loud and clear. "I'd like to go for a walk with my sister-in-law, Mr. Hall. If you wouldn't mind."

Juliet could taste the tension in the air, even though the two men were trying to hide it. Oh, she didn't have time for this.

"It certainly isn't my place to tell Mrs. Watts who she can stroll with."

"Just making sure." He extended a hand to Juliet. "How about it, Juliet? I'd like a chance to catch up and talk about Will—I mean, Hugh?"

———

"The first three or four years, I expected to see Will"—James dipped his chin in correction—"Hugh—every day. The longer time went, though, the surer I became."

Juliet listened to James's deep, somber voice as they walked the ranch. Cowboys were riding in now, the end of their day heralded by the sun slipping behind the mountains. James excused himself a few times to greet various men, get updates on the day's progress, make assignments for the next day.

Juliet watched him, running his ranch with authority and

confidence. So similar to Hugh in that respect. James was the outgoing brother, though, willing to rely on a joke and wink to gain a little ground. Hugh had preferred logic and reason.

She remembered *things* about him, but not the feelings anymore. They had all been laid to rest. *All* of her feelings—

Robert's kiss leaped to mind, accusing her of lying. He made her feel as if she was drowning, and it terrified her.

She turned away from those thoughts as James strode up. "So, what do you think of the place?"

Juliet hugged herself and looked around. "It's impressive."

The ranch was busy, productive. Bathed in the warm orange glow of sunset, cowboys unsaddled horses, groomed them, and turned them out for the night with whoops and smacks on the rumps. The moos and bawling of cattle filled the air with that needy urgency common to herd animals trying to stay together. The scent of biscuits and roast meat drifted in the air, working a grumble from her own stomach.

Two cowboys tossed a ball back and forth out in front of the bunkhouse. Romping horses off in the distance sent up a dust cloud that further softened the fall of twilight. The ranch was busy, but peaceful, and in this light had almost a storybook feel to it.

She and James drifted over to a corral fence and he rested his arms on the top rail, his gaze going out to the mountains in the distance. The sun, hidden by the tall peaks now, blazed behind them, turning the sky a dozen shades of orange and giving the mountains the illusion of fire. Juliet's arms tingled from either the coming chill or the beauty. She wasn't sure which.

"I don't know much about ranches, but it seems you've done a fine job with it. I'm sure Hugh—William—would be pleased."

James shook his head. "You don't even know what to call him, either. Heck of a thing." He pounded the rail lightly. "It's like you married a total stranger. A stranger to both of us."

"That's how I feel. I didn't know him. I only thought I did."

"I can understand why you're here. The questions must be driving you crazy."

"All these years, I just hated him, James. Hated him for being so...shallow. And now, I find out he was nothing but deep. The layers to him, to who he was, I can't even fathom. I just want answers. I want some peace."

He turned to her, seemed to drink her in for a moment. "I can see why he stayed in Texas. I wouldn't have left a pretty little thing like you either, especially to come live with a brother who couldn't decide if he wanted to forgive me or kill me."

Juliet didn't miss the stab at flattery. She expected James used the weapon quite efficiently, especially backed up with that roguish grin. But she was immune.

To him anyway.

She frowned at the subtle accusation from herself and focused on the conversation. She climbed up on the rail to watch horses milling around and ignore his gaze. "You didn't forgive him?"

"I told him I did...but a turncoat on the North? Honestly, I kept a mad on for a long time. What if we'd met on the battle-field? We could have killed each other." He pounded his fist on the corral rail again, harder. "Always thought when he came back we'd really hash it out and he'd explain it..."

Oh, Hugh, you left so much unfinished. Unsaid.

James lifted a strand of her hair. Juliet almost pulled away but didn't wish to be rude. As long as he wasn't. "I want you to know you're welcome here. I feel like this place is mine, but the fact is, it's just as much yours—"

"No, it isn't." She stepped down to face him, to put more space between them. "You've run it and built it up. I'm not here to make a claim. Besides, I have a saloon back in St. Joseph that I run." Although the prospect of returning to her old life now seemed lackluster. Devoid of purpose. The emptiness puzzled her.

James took her hand. His lids lowered a touch, that dangerous smile emerged. His voice softened to a huskier tone. "I thought my brother was the luckiest man in the world when he sent me that picture of you. I've been jealous ever since."

"Really?" she said, in no way hiding her sarcasm. "Please, James—" She attempted to pull away without being overtly rude.

"I had a wife. She didn't stay. She couldn't take the loneliness of ranch life. You could stay...and figure out things. Maybe get your questions answered."

His dark brown eyes held so many messages. Juliet had seen them before. This wasn't her first wrangle with a man who thought a suave smile and a few compliments opened *all* the doors. She pulled her hand away. "The offer is kind, but I don't know you and you don't know me—"

"Which is exactly the problem I'm trying to solve."

She laid her hand on his chest, setting the boundary. "Why don't we see if we can get to know your brother a little better first? Hmmm."

———

Robert tried focusing on the newspaper articles, but his mind was outside with Juliet and James. He would pay good money to be a fly on the wall for that conversation. James Watts was indeed a womanizer, and he was setting his sights on his brother's widow.

To what end?

Because he was lonely and she was beautiful? Or he wanted to make sure *his* ranch wasn't in jeopardy of switching hands. More questions, but Robert guessed a little of both.

Frustrated, he rose and strode to the door, absently bringing a couple of the newspaper articles with him. James had left the door open and Robert could see him and Juliet, strolling, stopping to chat with the hands as they rode in. Robert didn't trust this man any more than he trusted his superiors in Washington. Everyone involved with Watts had an agenda, it seemed. Some obvious, some less so.

And Robert Hall was no different, he reminded himself. While he was tremendously curious about Hugh Watts's secrets, he really only cared about Juliet—

He gulped in shock as James took her hand in his. *The man doesn't waste any time.*

Burning with jealousy, and freely admitting it, Robert watched James pull Juliet closer. He had the irrational desire to burst out there and interrupt them—

But Juliet laid her hand on the man's chest and Robert smiled. "Atta girl," he whispered. He knew that stance—the raised chin, slightly tilted head, squared shoulders. There was no affection in the move. She was putting the man in his place—

"Fire! The barn's on fire!"

Every head on the ranch swiveled. Robert rushed to the edge of the porch, shoving the articles in his pocket. A young cowboy erupted from the barn, eyes wide, face flushed. "Get the buckets," he screamed.

Robert didn't hesitate. He joined the swarm of men racing to the barn. A man appeared among them, a dozen buckets hanging on his arms, and he began passing them out as two lines of cowboys formed on each side of the water trough. The buckets instantly started circulating from the trough, down the line of sweating, racing men, to inside the shadows of the barn. Robert jumped in beside Juliet as James raced inside to assess things.

Robert could smell smoke. Suddenly, it lurched out the door and through the opening in the hay loft like a train's smoke stack. He took a full bucket from Juliet, exchanged it for an empty one. Bucket after bucket rotated through their hands. Several horses thundered from the barn, followed by James waving one arm at the animals, and carrying a saddle in the other.

He dropped the tack and hollered at his men, "Keep that water coming!" With that, he disappeared inside the building, emerging over and over with horses or tack. The fire brigade kept up its frantic pace, and shortly, Robert noticed the smoke slowing. "I think we're getting a handle on it."

Juliet passed him a bucket. "I hope so." Full dark had settled now, but someone had lit a lantern hanging on a post. The weak light cast eerie, desperate shadows around them.

Several minutes later, James emerged from the barn one last time, streaks of soot across his face, his shirt and pants soaked from spills, a smoking saddle blanket in his right hand. "Just a few more ought to do it." He turned back to the shadows, "Dan, make sure that back stall gets a good soaking. Don't come outta there till you're sure there's nothing smoldering." James strode up to the trough, tossed away the blanket, and shouldered through his men. "Thanks, boys." He splashed water on his face, dipped his hands again, and ran them through his hair.

Dan, a pudgy, short man, jogged out of the barn, two empty buckets swinging in his hands. "I think that's got it, boss. Maybe just a couple more."

James nodded. "All right. Good." He waved at the line of firefighters on both sides of him. "Shut her down." To Dan, he said, "Let me know what started it, if you can."

Dan traded a cowboy for two full buckets, but then the fire brigade reversed direction. Robert followed the lead of the other men and dumped his water back into the trough, as did Juliet. In the faint light, a fat but spry little man went down the line gathering up buckets. Apparently, he was a sort of fire chief, and it looked like he'd done his job well, judging by the relief reflected on James's face.

The rancher drifted through his men, slapping them on

their backs, thanking them. He came to Robert and offered his hand. "Thank you. I appreciate you jumping in like that." He winked at Juliet. "Both of you."

"Couldn't do any less," Robert said, appreciating the man's gratitude.

"We caught it in time?" Juliet asked.

"Pretty much. Mostly lost some hay, scorched a stall pretty good, but I think it'll be all right." He shot his gaze between their shoulders. "Lucky, take Clem and go round up those horses." An older man with long, gray hair tapped the brim of his hat in confirmation.

James started back for his house and Robert and Juliet fell in behind him. "I could use a drink," he said, crossing the porch. Just inside the kitchen door, he lit a wall lantern and used its glow to navigate into the parlor just beyond, Juliet and Robert following—

Robert nearly skidded to a stop. He spun back to the kitchen, eliciting a shocked expression from Juliet. The kitchen table was empty. Robert raced up to it and slapped his hands down on the wood. Bare wood. He couldn't believe his eyes. The simple, round pine table was empty. All of the newspaper articles, the photo, and the satchel were gone.

Chapter Twenty-Two

Juliet and James walked up behind Robert and he grasped at a rational hope. "Do you have a housekeeper, James? Did she clear the table?"

"Nooo," James whispered, then louder, "I don't understand. Are you saying all those items from the safe deposit box are gone?" He reached past Robert and turned up the lamp hanging over the table, spilling light everywhere.

"I left them right here. On this table. Do you have a house-keeper or anyone who would have cleared the table?"

"No. No one comes in here but me, besides, everybody would have been outside at the fire."

"The fire," Robert whispered, a horrible realization dawning on him. "The fire was a distraction."

James dropped his hands on his hips and stared at the table. "Maybe. Fires happen. Especially in a barn. I'll go question all the men, though. See if any of them came in here for some reason, or if they saw anybody around the barn, or here in the house."

"Good. Yes." But Robert knew what had happened. When James closed the door, he looked at Juliet. "I think we were followed. And I only told one person we were coming to Defiance." Anger ignited in him like a match burst. He cursed and hit the table, making her jump. "I have been so stupid. All of this, the whole time, I think Senator Wilson has been behind the entire investigation."

"Why? What's he after?"

Robert wanted to let loose with a primal scream of rage. If he could only answer that one question. To keep from hitting the table again, he shoved his hands into his pockets and felt the crumpled newspaper articles. "I was holding these when the kid yelled fire." Praying there was a reason he still had them, he smoothed them out on the table and he and Juliet leaned in close to read them.

One article heralded *Colfax Elected Speaker of the House of Representatives*. "He was implicated in the Credit Mobilier scandal." Nothing in the article leaped out at Robert. The second item, however, froze his blood. A grainy photograph of several men in suits, faces all but obscured by time and bushy beards, included a short story below it. *Luncheon to Benefit Wounded Veterans*. The article was innocuous enough, but Robert finally saw an important connection.

"What is it?"

His excitement—or his loathing—must have shown. "War-hero and candidate for Maryland's House of Representatives, General Desmond Wilson joined representatives Oakes Ames, Schuyler Colfax, James Brooks, and several local dignitaries for a luncheon today to benefit wounded veterans." He skimmed the article, reading the pertinent points. "Wilson's name has been bandied about for other potential opportunities...popular enough to win the Senate...strong proponent of a transcontinental railroad..."

"What do you see?"

"Every one of those men—except for Wilson—was implicated in the Credit Mobilier scandal. And he won the Senate seat in 1874."

The connections, the links were there, but he just couldn't

wind them together in a single, cohesive strand. "Maxwe—
Hugh—he was from Maryland."

"His brother said so, yes."

Ideas, theories, and scenarios roared through Robert's
brain. "What if Hugh had some information on Wilson.
Potentially damaging information. Wilson would want to
know its status. He'd want it in his own hands, but he lost
Hugh until a few days before the Comanche attack. Then he
hears Hugh is dead, but that he had a wife. A wife he may have
shared information with. But then he loses track of you."

"So, he kept looking for me."

"*I* was looking for you." He straightened up and turned to
her. "And they were watching me. Somehow they pieced my
work together and found you. But my investigation was never
official. It couldn't be traced back to them or Wilson. Merely
an open file..." If he'd only let her go. He wanted to kick
himself for dragging her into all this.

"But why would they care? If Hugh had this dangerous,
explosive information, if it implicated Wilson in the Credit
Mobilier scandal, that's all passed now—"

"It could still cost him his career, like it did Ames."
Robert's last conversation with Wilson echoed in his brain.

"*I want you to go to St. Joe and investigate. If you still think she
knows nothing of her husband's activities, we'll close the file and let it
be. Mrs. Juliet Watts can disappear again. But I need at least very
strong circumstantial evidence.*"

"If we hadn't found that key, I would have reported you
didn't know anything about Hugh's past, and all this would
have never happened. I think the senator truly wanted to close
the file on you. And now he can't. It's all my fault. If I'd just
left you—"

She squeezed his arm and her touch jolted him. "It's not
your fault. It may not even be Hugh's fault. If Wilson did
something illegal, then all this is his fault. And he shouldn't get
away with it."

James stomped in and shut the door hard behind him. "I'll stand by my men. None of them know anything about stolen papers. But Dan caught sight of a dapple tied out near the back corral. He was coming to ask me about it when Shoyo yelled *fire*."

Robert chewed on the news for a moment. The implication was obvious. "Someone's watching us. We'll have to be careful tomorrow. If we find anything, don't tip our hand."

———

Juliet had not done any serious horseback riding in about five years. A terrible storm had flooded nearly everything in St. Joe in '72 and stranded her whiskey shipment. Since every wagon in town was out on rescue missions, she and Sam had simply ridden horses and brought along a mule to save the driver and her liquor.

The horses had waded through icy, muddy water up to their bellies. Early spring, the weather had been cold, gray, and dismal. Asked if she ever wanted to ride again, she would have said no...until today.

James's ranch offered some of the most breathtaking views she had ever seen. At one point, they climbed a mountain and the world seemed to fall away. The horizon went on for miles, filled with ridge after ridge of jagged, blue, snow-tipped mountains. The creak of the leather and the scream of a hawk had been the only sounds on the wind, and she understood now the affection James had for these mountains.

"St. Joe. The Chesapeake Bay." James rode up beside her. "They don't hold much in the way of beauty when you've seen a view like this."

"I'd be inclined to agree."

She noticed Robert didn't say anything, but he did look to be enjoying the view.

"But I brought you up here for more than sightseeing." They rounded a bend in the trail and a sudden, almost-dizzying 360-degree view of the valley unfolded beneath them. They pulled up beside each other and James motioned out in front of them. "From here, you can see the whole ranch. This is where William and I were standing when he decided to homestead here."

Robert whistled. "Where do we start?"

James squinted and pointed down, almost directly below them. "That section right there. That clearing. That's the original homestead section. A trapper had built a cabin there, but by the time we came along, wasn't anything left but the chimney. We rebuilt—" James stopped, tilted his head, and whispered, "The chimney..."

"What?" Did Juliet dare hope for a clue?

"The first night we camped here, William found the remnants of a hymnal kinda tucked back in the chimney." James smiled at the memory. "He tossed it at me and said maybe I could sing him to sleep. Well, that was a big joke because I'm tone deaf. Pa always said when I sang, dogs howled"—he cut his eyes over to Juliet and Robert—"and rocks cried out. I never knew what he meant. It's from the Bible."

———

Juliet forgot all about the views and her saddle-weary rear end as they hurried down a fairly rugged trail, crossed two streams, and finally, an hour later, came out in a clearing that was slowly being taken over by aspens and wild flowers. The cabin was little more than a dilapidated, one-room box with tiny, broken windows, but they were all excited to see it.

James kicked his horse into a trot and she and Robert followed. He rode up to the porch, swung from the saddle, and barreled into the front door—which firmly rejected his attempt to enter. Hanging at a noticeable angle, it didn't look as if it had been opened in years.

"Dang," James whispered, tightening his grip on the door-knob. "I'll get this." He slammed his shoulder into it and it opened, protesting with a scream.

The three of them entered the cabin with caution. The sounds of mice skittering across the wood and the unmistakable rattle of a Diamondback somewhere beneath them prompted Robert and James to pull their guns. Juliet gathered in her skirts to better see the floor around her. Overhead in the loft, something larger scrambled for a hiding place.

As far as furniture, all that remained in the cabin was a small, square table, without any accompanying chairs, and one fruit box resting on a warped slab that had once acted as a counter.

James approached the fireplace and let out a long sigh. He surveyed it carefully then dropped his Colt back into its holster. "Keep an eye out for that snake, will ya?"

Robert nodded and James stepped forward. He drifted his hands over the smooth, river rock, tugging occasionally, checking for loose stones. Eventually, he worked his way back to one that touched the wall. They all heard the sound of crumbling mortar and rocks scraping. An instant later, he dropped the stone on the ground. Its removal left a dark hole in the chimney and Juliet saw the straight edge of something that wasn't a rock.

Swallowing, James tugged on the object and waited, apparently for a snake. He tugged again, and now Juliet could see the edge of a leather envelope. Convinced the item wasn't protected by the rattler, James hauled it out and showed it to them. A dusty leather portfolio, roughly a foot square, tied with a leather string.

James hurried over to the table, undid the tie, and dumped the contents on the table.

Chapter Twenty-Three

An envelope, a journal, and stock certificates for the Union Pacific Railroad spilled onto the table. Robert immediately recognized the emblem for the Pinkerton agency on the envelope. As Juliet reached for the journal, he plucked the envelope from the table and opened it.

He scanned it and knew, almost immediately, it answered one important question. "Hugh was a spy for the Union."

Juliet looked at the paper in his hands. "What is that?"

"Orders. During the war, intelligence operations were mostly directed by General McClellan. He hired Allen Pinkerton to direct operations and gather information. These orders instruct Hugh to infiltrate a company of Confederate soldiers that would be transporting munitions from Richmond to Charleston. He was supposed to sabotage the train, make sure it never got there."

"So..." James shrugged a shoulder. "He didn't change sides?"

"Maybe not." Robert still had to piece everything together to answer that definitively.

"What happened then?" James pressed. "I know the train ran into Union troops. It blew up. Soldiers—Union and Confederate—were killed, but Hugh was blamed as a traitor.

So, he ran to avoid getting hung? But he told me there were no munitions aboard. Instead, they were transporting a passenger. A VIP. And that's all he ever said."

"The rest of the story is right here." Juliet collapsed back against the counter. She had paled considerably and was breathing faster as she scanned and flipped the first few pages. "Hugh saw the passenger." She looked up at Robert. "General Desmond Wilson." Robert shouldn't have been surprised, but was. The one man he'd thought—

"Hugh recognized him," Juliet continued, "mistakenly thought he was being kidnapped and tried to rescue him.

"Hugh had already set the bomb and was trying to get Wilson off the train when the Union troops boarded it. Wilson forced Hugh at gunpoint to get him away safely without warning the troops. And he forced him to escort him to Charleston."

She flipped more pages, hurriedly scanning the text. "On the way to Charleston, Wilson explained to Hugh that whoever won the war, a transcontinental railroad was going to be built. Either the North would do it, or the South would. Whoever it turned out to be, Wilson wanted friends in both camps....um, to that end, he was going to Charleston to meet with Jefferson Davis and make a good-faith effort toward a strategic alliance... He was going to give Davis high-level intelligence on Gen. Grant's final assault... Davis would offer Wilson a commission in the Confederate army if he, for some reason, needed to leave the North... Wilson was quite sure a similar offer could be extended to Hugh, if he was inclined to trade loyalties."

Juliet skimmed silently for a few more minutes, then continued her summary. "Wilson told Hugh he'd introduce him to Davis as an aide-de-camp. This would earn him a return trip with Wilson to Washington.

"Or, Wilson would turn him over to Davis as a spy and let the president ship him off to Andersonville.

"Hugh says he agreed to switch sides only in an effort to get back to the North and share this intelligence with Pinkerton...but Wilson was prepared for that. When he and Hugh crossed from Virginia into Maryland, they were met by Thomas Durant, who Wilson said would be a witness against Hugh if Hugh backed out or tried to tell the truth about any of this. Wilson promised he would smear Hugh as a *Confederate* spy...Wilson also would transfer *James* to the worst fighting possible if Hugh backed out..."

She scanned more pages, her fingers skimming across the paper. Robert couldn't believe the lengths Wilson had gone to for a piece of the railroad pie. Eleven men had died in that train explosion.

Juliet continued. "Hugh said he panicked, stole the valise Wilson was carrying so he'd have some kind of proof, and ran. He didn't stop running till he made it to Texas."

Robert pursed his lips, his heart bruised with the betrayal. "Wilson. All this time. Wilson. He's had access to everything I've done. Every clue I turned over looking for you. And while that story is enlightening, unfortunately, it's also only heresy. The word of a dead man against a US Senator."

Juliet opened a sheet of paper tucked in the journal, read it with a solemn expression, and passed it to Robert. "This might change your mind."

Robert read it and let out an astonished whistle. "The offer to Wilson of a commission in the Confederacy. And it's signed by Jefferson Davis himself."

James grimaced with disgust. "Are you saying he had the proof that a United States senator was a traitor? And he just hid it? Why?"

"It was a Mexican stand-off." Robert slapped the orders against his palm. "As long as Hugh had the valise, Wilson couldn't risk doing anything to him or you, and Wilson couldn't go after Hugh for fear he'd release the information to Pinkerton." Robert kept slapping the paper and commenced to pacing the floor. "Wilson didn't run for his first public office until '67, the year Hugh died. He served two years in Congress, kept a low profile, but actively supported the railroad. He ran for and won the Senate in '74 and has been raising his profile little by little ever since. Testing the waters. Trying, I think, to find out if this information was going to surface. He wasn't tied publicly to the Credit Mobilier scandal. I think he was cautiously optimistic that he never would be, especially with Hugh's death." He looked at Juliet. "Until he knew what you knew, he couldn't ever be sure."

"But he *was* involved in the scandal, look." James held up the railroad certificates. "These are Wilson's, signed by Durant."

"I think Hugh was trying to protect you and Juliet by holding on to all this. Inadvertently, he prompted Wilson to take a more cautious approach to politics. He avoided any connection with the Credit Mobilier mess and looked like an innocent babe, in part, because Hugh hid the paper trail."

"And you think he did that to *protect* us, not blackmail Wilson?" Hope lit Juliet's face.

Robert strode over and looked deeply into her eyes, trying to offer some peace, some closure. "Initially, this was about protecting himself and James. Then you came along. And I think Hugh knew exactly what he was doing when he hid that key in your locket. I think as long as he had this information hidden away, all of you were safe from Wilson."

"He wants to be president."

Robert blinked and rounded on James. The weight of the statement stunned him. "How do you know that?"

"At the state convention last month, the delegates were given a secret ballot. Names of potential presidential nominees. Wilson's was top of the list."

This was not information Robert wanted and he paced the floor, thinking, planning. "I have to assume that information raises the stakes significantly. Maybe that's been Wilson's goal all along." The man had been known for his long-term planning during the war. He'd won several battles because he was patient, never jumped the gun, or rushed his men. "First, we have to assume whoever stole the satchel is still nearby. We have to lose him and get to Defiance. I have a contact in the Pinkerton office in Denver. Someone besides us needs to see all this information."

Juliet wore a blank expression, as if she simply couldn't comprehend the impact of what Hugh had done...or the depth of her misconceptions about him.

"Forgive me. For years, the two of you didn't know what kind of a man Hugh was. This must be welcome but jarring news. The locket held the key to his insurance. Your safety."

Juliet drifted out to the porch and Robert kicked himself mentally. For a decade, she'd thought her dead husband a shallow scoundrel. Instead, he'd carried a secret to his grave that had kept her safe.

James watched her leave as well, holding his peace until she was outside. Then he exhaled a long, sad breath. "Now I wish I would have said I forgive him with a little more sincerity. Must have been hard to keep all this to himself...not tell anyone, especially her." He chuckled, but it was a sad sound. "He wrote me one letter, no return address, but he told me about her. He was crazy in love. Said she made him feel like he was drowning."

"She has that effect," Robert muttered and immediately regretted the slip.

James cut his eyes at him. "Yeah. I suspected as much."

———

Well, there it was. Juliet sat down on the edge of the sagging porch and stared out at the mountains rising over the tops of the pines. *All these years I wasted nursing a phantom grudge, holding on to a lie...and he was protecting us. He did it out of love.*

And God, You had this worked out from the beginning, but I couldn't see...couldn't trust...

A sob tried to work free but she fought it back. It escaped, instead, in tears, hot and salty. Robert sat down beside her. She quickly turned away and wiped her cheeks. A futile effort, as the tears wouldn't stop.

"Juliet."

She couldn't look at him. She hadn't cried over Hugh or even her loneliness in who knew how long. She didn't want anyone to see this pain. This regret.

"Juliet," he said more insistently and touched her shoulder.

Her walls fell and she suddenly found herself crying—no sobbing—into his shoulder. He held her tight, pressed his lips to the top of her head, and whispered, "Shhh. It's all right now."

"I let it eat me up inside. I hated him. I hated God. I just wanted to be left alone and never hope, or love, or get hurt again. And I've lost ten years hiding in my saloon. A hermit surrounded by people."

"Well, it's a good thing His mercies are new every day. Maybe you did lose a decade hiding from life. Hiding your heart. But today is a new day, Juliet." He lifted her face to him. His throat rippled for a moment, his jaw tightened, and his eyes burned brightly, like a thousand fires glowed deep in his soul. "Let the rest of your life start right now."

She sniffled and the question that cried out for an answer came to her again. "Why did you look for me for ten years?"

His shoulders sagged a little, but his expression hardened, as if he was resigned to something. "Because I couldn't forget you. I tried. Hard as I knew how, I tried. But God told me to hang on. He led me to believe He would bring you back into my life. Why do you think I held on to the locket? I knew I'd see you again."

He hesitated a moment then lowered his lips, but not all the way. He paused, a breath from her lips. She understood and couldn't deny her need, her hunger for him. She closed the distance, pressing her lips to his, completing the kiss. Peace, relief, *love* cascaded over Juliet like a waterfall, refilling her heart with emotions she hadn't risked in so long.

She wanted to run in the sunshine, throw out her arms and laugh, and spin in a circle till she was crazy dizzy. She wanted to breathe deeply, laugh often, and love with abandon.

Robert kissed her long and deep, possessively, and she kissed him the same way. No more ambiguities. No more guesses. She didn't know where this kiss would take her, but she was done hiding.

"Uh, I hate to interrupt..." James stood in the doorway of the shack, studying a knothole in the frame. Only slightly embarrassed, Juliet and Robert pulled apart. "But, like you said," James continued, "we have to assume we're being watched. And I think it should look like we're leaving here with empty hands." He tapped his stomach and it gave back a distinctively flat sound.

––––––

On the way back to the ranch, the three rode at a leisurely pace and even stopped at another old shack to look around. Robert kept a watchful eye out, but never caught sign of anyone spying. If someone was there, he was subtle and keeping his distance. The fire at the ranch had the earmarks of a Pinkerton tactic. With an office in Denver, they could have dispatched several agents. Robert suspected, though, only one was on Wilson's private payroll. He prayed he was right.

Getting past one man would be much easier, and he and Juliet planned to slip away in the dead of night. James surreptitiously saddled fresh horses and had them ready at midnight. He met Robert and Juliet behind the barn with the mounts.

The fingernail moon didn't offer much light, but Juliet could see well enough to spot the mischief in James's gleaming grin. He held her bay still as she planted her foot in the stir-rup. "I will miss you, you know. Come back when you can stay longer."

Deciding it would be better to say goodbye to him from the saddle, she hoisted herself up, only a little surprised at where he put his hands to assist her. She doubted he could see the smirk on her face, but they both knew it was there. "I suppose I'll miss you some, too, James. I don't know if I could have gotten in the saddle by myself."

He chuckled and stepped back. "And I will miss your sass."

She huffed her disapproval, then softened. "Seriously, I do hope to come back by someday. I'd like to learn more about Hugh—when he was William."

He paused before he answered, and she heard appreciation in his voice. "You are welcome anytime. But at least we know what matters. He was a good man."

Before she could respond, he slapped her horse's neck and stepped over to Robert's horse. "Take off outta here slow and easy. Don't do anything to spook the herd and you won't draw any attention to yourself. Hopefully, in the morning, our guest will realize you're long gone, and you'll be on the train to Denver."

"Thanks, James."

"No, thank you." The two men shook hands. "I appreciate you're gonna clear my brother's name. I don't know if I'll change back to Maxwell, but it'll be nice knowing I can."

Chapter Twenty-Four

Robert was feeling lighter and freer than he had in years, despite the grueling ride in the dark to the Animas Forks train station. Once aboard, an exhausted Juliet had slept peacefully beside him on the train, her head on his shoulder much of the time. He leaned over more than once and planted a light kiss on the top of her head. He couldn't see the future. He didn't know if they had one together, but they were at the start of something, and he was most definitely *encouraged*.

Surprisingly, by the time they pulled into Denver at three in the afternoon, Robert's mood had turned. Tension crawled up his spine. He was anxious, but about what, he couldn't say.

The Credit Mobilier scandal was going to take down yet another crooked politician, perhaps the most audacious one of all, bearing in mind his presidential aspirations. Could it be as easy as turning over a satchel to a Pinkerton agent? Why didn't he think so?

Beside him, Juliet stretched in her seat and smiled at him. "I'd like to go a long time without riding on a train. The seats leave something to be desired."

He leaned toward her and rested his elbow on the armrest. "Prefer another day in the saddle?"

"From here to St. Joe would be an awfully long ride."

Yes, she did have a home to go to. Of course she did. What was he thinking? He tried to hide his disappointment, foolish as it was, and sat back on the seat. "St. Joe." Just where did he think she was going to go?

"It's my home. I have a business there."

"Yes, I'm...of course, you have to go back." He had to say something more than that.

"I feel a little lost now, to be honest. I *don't* feel much like hiding anymore. The Lost Sally was my cave...it seems small now. Pointless." She shook her head. "I don't know. I just have this funny, restless feeling, and I don't know where it's coming from."

He swiped a hand over his face. So many things he wanted to tell her, ask her, invite her into. Was she thirsty enough? "What do you want, Juliet?" He held her gaze, willed her not to look away.

Her mouth moved wordlessly for a moment before she finally managed, "I—I'm not sure. What do you want?" she asked hesitantly.

"I've had ten years to think about it. I think I know what I want."

"Denver, ten minutes!" The conductor shouted over their heads as he ambled down the aisle, breaking the spell. Robert sighed, reprimanded himself for not focusing on business.

"Juliet, we're going to go to the Pinkerton office when we get off the train. Alex Danbury is the head detective. I know him from his time in the Army. They'll help us get Hugh's information"—he tapped the satchel sitting in his lap—"to the attorney general. He's the only one with the authority to investigate a sitting senator.

"But I also think we should send a summary of what's going on to several newspapers. They could put a lot of pressure on the government to go after Wilson. He's a very powerful senator with powerful friends."

"Can you trust Danbury?"

"Unless he's had a lobotomy, yes. The man was straight and true to a fault. Highly ethical and reliable. He'll help us get this information in the right hands."

"And then?"

And then? I'll ask you to marry me, Juliet. I'll tell you how much I love you and how I thought of you every day for a decade. You'll fall into my arms and we'll live happily ever after. Instead, trying to sound lighthearted, he said, "Maybe you'd let me buy you dinner at Delmonico's. To finish talking about what we want. And we do have a lot to celebrate."

"You solved a case. We can celebrate that. But for me, it feels more like giving thanks. I'm grateful. I'm grateful I was wrong about Hugh. I'm grateful you held on to that stupid locket. I'm grateful"—she smiled at him—"that you never gave up on me. You were unwavering."

He couldn't help himself. He turned to face her again and touched her cheek, drifted his thumb across her lips. "I can honestly say you were worth the commitment."

The train jolted and the whistle blew, announcing Denver.

Robert sat back and prayed simply, *Please, Lord, make her thirsty...for us both.*

———

Leery, but allowing that he was probably just being paranoid, Robert helped Juliet off the train while watching the crowd of passengers and greeters. The station swarmed with happy families, young lovers, a small contingent of soldiers, and a short parade of traveling salesmen in loud suits carrying suitcases and wheeling trunks filled with their wares.

As Robert pulled Juliet through the crowd, he told her over his shoulder, "The office is on West Street. We'll walk. It's not far."

"All right, but as soon as we can, I want a room and a bath."

"You'll be putting that off for a bit, dear." The sultry, feminine voice set off alarm bells in Robert's head, even before he felt the blunt steel of a gun barrel pressed to his ribs.

He stopped abruptly. Juliet stared, puzzled at first, but her expression suddenly melted into one of understanding as her eyes ricocheted from the woman to the gun in her hand, not quite hidden by her shawl.

A stunning brunette—no doubt the one who had so entranced Mr. Fenton at the First Bank of Nashville—shoved the gun deeper into Robert's ribs. He winced slightly.

"Try anything and an innocent bystander could get hurt."

"I'll go with you. I won't give you any trouble, but leave her here."

Simultaneously, both women balked. "I can't." "She will not."

The woman added, "Like you, she's one of the guests of honor."

———

A quick ride in a cab—at gunpoint—was not how Robert had seen this day going. At least the information on Wilson was safe. He clutched the satchel on his lap. Now, if only he could keep Juliet safe.

"I presume you are the other Mrs. Watts?"

Juliet's catty question elicited a slight upturn of the woman's lips. "For all the good it did me."

"How did you know we'd be here?" Robert asked.

"A telegram from the operative who followed you to the ranch. You slipped away in the night. That meant you found something. You'd be on your way here to either turn it over to a Pinkerton or take it on to Washington."

"Who are you? A Pinkerton or...?" Robert asked.

"I am a longtime and trusted associate of Senator Wilson's. We go back several years."

Longtime? "The woman on the train." Robert suddenly knew it without needing any proof. "You were on the train that night."

She shrugged lazily. "Someone had to stay behind. Someone had to make sure that word reached the right people that William Maxwell was a traitor if the story became necessary. I also planted the story that General Wilson's short disappearance was due to a mild bout with malaria."

"Wilson was going to betray Maxwell the whole time."

"He knew Maxwell hadn't truly switched sides, but it didn't matter. We had a smear campaign in place. No one would believe a lowly private over a general."

"Hugh knew it, too," Juliet said. "That was why he ran. So he could think, make a plan. He was deliberate."

The woman frowned. "Annoyingly so." An instant later, the cab rolled to a stop in front of the luxury Denver House hotel and her expression lightened instantly. "Finally, we can be done with this."

Chapter Twenty-Five

The woman ushered Robert and Juliet into a suite. Juliet couldn't help but marvel for an instant over the accommodations. A lodging befitting of a king, not an American senator. A fire roared in the mammoth fireplace. The chairs and the oversized settee were covered in velvet and satin.

A stunning array of Indian artifacts lined the glistening mahogany paneling. Skins, spears, shields, bows, and arrows surrounded them. No doubt a valuable collection, Juliet assumed. Fit for a museum. Regardless, the arrows made her shiver.

A large man in an expensive suit stood at the bar, pouring himself a drink. "Well, Robert, it's good to see you." He capped the decanter and rounded on them. "And the elusive Mrs. Watts." He strode over to them. "You are a sight for these weary, worried eyes. I thought we might never find you and I'd spend my life wondering if you were going to ruin my career at any moment." He tossed back the liquor. "I cannot tell you how good it feels to have that monkey off my back."

Her heart pounding in her chest like war drums, Juliet offered no response.

"Senator Wilson—" Robert took a step forward. Simultaneously, Wilson took one back and the woman circled around in front of them, placing herself between Robert and the senator.

The woman waved her .38 at Robert. "Aaah aaah ah. Keep your distance."

Sweat bathed Juliet's palms. If there was only something she could do...

Pray, an inner voice whispered.

She did, willingly, eagerly. She prayed for protection for Robert, for some kind of divine intervention, a way out of this situation.

"Pardon my manners, Robert. Mrs. Watts. This is my associate Millicent." When neither Robert nor Juliet responded, the man shrugged and returned to his bar for another drink. "Give me everything you found on that god-forsaken ranch. Make this easy and you and Mrs. Watts can walk out of here."

He sounded almost bored.

"I don't have anything," Robert said.

Senator Wilson sighed, threw back his second drink, then slammed the snifter down on the marble-topped bar. "I don't have time for games, Robert. I need to get back to Washington. Now I know you have something you were going to give to the Pinkertons. We intercepted your telegram from Defiance."

"I don't have anything," he repeated slowly, firmly.

Senator Wilson glared at him with narrowed, angry eyes. Fear slithered in Juliet's stomach. The senator was dangerous. As was this Millicent. "What did you find on that ranch?" the politician demanded softly.

"The orders sending Hugh—*Maxwell*—off to infiltrate the company moving that ammunition. Which turned out to be, of course, a cover. They were moving you."

"And the letter to me from Jefferson Davis?"

"It was with Hugh's confession."

"Confession?" Wilson mumbled a curse under his breath. "A confession *and* the letter?"

"And Hugh's orders, and the railroad stocks signed over to you," Robert said, reciting the inventory of their find.

"Well, you've just got the whole shooting match." He took a menacing step toward them, his presence growing larger.

Robert wasn't afraid, Juliet knew for certain, but he turned his head a touch, as if acknowledging her presence. No, he wasn't afraid for himself, but he was for her, and she hated that she was leverage for Wilson.

"I'll ask again, Robert, hand it over."

Robert hesitated. "I encoded my telegram to Danbury. He got on the train in Bailey. We passed each other in the aisle, exchanged satchels, and now your whole treasonous, illegal history is on its way to Washington. It should be delivered to the attorney general at a secret location sometime in the next few days."

Wilson sputtered. His face flushed. Juliet had seen a thousand drunks build to an eruption in just this way. An explosion was coming.

Oh, God, please, God, keep Robert safe...

Chapter Twenty-Six

Wilson roared like an enraged bull and snatched the satchel out from under Robert's arm. Robert sent up a quick prayer as the politician tore open the bag and pulled out a handful of shredded newspapers. Disbelieving, he fished deeper, frantically, coming up with the same result, littering the floor with the trash.

For an instant, Millicent's eyes shot to Wilson and her brow dove. Robert lunged. He intended to grab the gun, but in the scramble, it went flying. Millicent howled like a banshee and clawed at Robert. He jabbed her in the jaw, without any regrets, and knocked her out. Before she hit the floor, he spun, intent on grabbing the gun. Juliet was already racing for it. Wilson had dropped the satchel and was lunging for it as well. She couldn't beat him to it but managed to kick it away, back toward Robert.

Good girl!

He and Wilson both eyed the weapon then each other. Robert, younger, faster, more desperate, lunged for the Colt. Wilson reached out, snatched a Cheyenne arrow off the wall, and stabbed with it like a knife as Robert came up with the gun. The tip sank deep into his chest. Juliet screamed. Robert ignored the searing pain, clutched the arrow to stop it from sinking any deeper, and fired the revolver.

Wilson stumbled back against the wall, blood exploding from his left shoulder. Robert fired again, placing the shot in Wilson's right shoulder. His left hand, slick with blood, yanked the arrow free. Barely noticing the pain, he cocked the revolver. "The next one kills you, Senator. Your choice." His voice was raspy, breathless, and it surprised him.

Hate and rage roiled the old man's face. His cheeks flushed so red, Robert thought he might have an apoplectic fit right there, but slowly, he turned his sweat-slicked palms out in surrender. "Get me a doctor." He slithered to the ground. "Quick."

Juliet raced to Robert's side, tears spilling down her cheeks, and pawed at his shirt. "Let me see, let me see." Her voice was choked and he ached at the fear he heard, even as his legs grew weak.

"It's not that bad," he assured her. *Is it?* With his bloody hand, he clutched her fingers to still them, met her eyes for a moment, but kept the gun trained on Wilson. "Yours was worse—"

"But you're bleeding." She tugged his shirt tail free and pressed it to the wound, gasping as he sank to his knees. "Oh, God," she cried, "Please, Robert, please don't—"

"I'll live. I promise, I'll live." *Won't I, Lord? You didn't bring me this far just to...* His vision fogged, his head swam. "You keep an eye on Millicent there, Juliet."

"I—I," she stammered. "You have to be all right."

"Millicent, Juliet. And have faith—I'm in God's hands."

He heard a frantic pounding on the door and several panicked voices heralded the arrival of help. *Good.* The door burst open and Robert vaguely saw moving forms through a rising darkness. *Good. Now I can sleep...*

He closed his eyes now. "Robert." Juliet's tear-soaked voice followed him into the darkness... "Robert..."

Chapter Twenty-Seven

❧

"And that, Sam, is how the story ends." Juliet pushed the beer away. She didn't drink much anyway, and right now it didn't have a chance at making her feel better. "All those years I thought the worst of Hugh, and he was a hero. He kept his brother and me safe. Now the information will shut down Wilson. He's been bribing and blackmailing people in Washington since the first year of the war. A lot of people are going to go to jail."

"And they might not have caught him if it hadn't been for your husband." Sam dropped to his elbows on the bar. His old, grizzled face was kind and gentle. "Terrible way he died, but at least the good Lord didn't let him die in vain."

Juliet thought of the silly story of Sean Flynn. How Robert wouldn't have worried about the fight if he'd known the man better. How Juliet should have trusted the Lord, accepting that He was sovereign over everything.

"I am definitely"—she smiled, remembering Sean Flynn—"getting to know Him, Sam."

He grinned, so big and wide his wrinkles nearly shut his eyes. "Now that does my heart good to hear." He stood up again, threw the bar towel over his shoulder. "One thing I don't understand, Miss Juliet. What are you doing here?"

Juliet wasn't sure she understood the question. "It's my bar. It's my home. Where else was I going to go?"

"What about that fella? Robert?"

"Oh, well, we talked a little but..." It seemed he was waiting on something, but Juliet couldn't quite pin it down. "He's already out of the hospital. But, umm, he said he had a lot of work to do in Washington. He has to close this case. Depositions and more investigations to see who else is involved. He's going to be very busy for the next few months. Maybe longer."

One of Sam's eyebrows dove, expressing skepticism. "The man looked for you for ten years."

What did he want her to say? She couldn't explain exactly why she was here. Robert hadn't tried to stop her from coming home. She straightened up and slapped the bar. "I'm going to go finish unpacking. I'll come down and help you with the rush."

Empty, lost, devoid of any fire, she started to leave, but Sam's gentle voice stopped her. "Seems to me, he's said everything you should need to hear. Sometimes, you gotta meet a man halfway, Miss Juliet."

She rounded on her old friend. "And shouldn't he be brave enough, man enough, to spell things out for me? He could've told me he didn't want me to leave. He didn't say anything." Maybe he shouldn't have had to. *Maybe he was waiting on me? Can I be that thick?* "Did he say it and I just didn't hear?"

"Lead a horse to water, Lord," Sam muttered, sounding thoroughly disgusted with her. "Sounds to me like he said a lot. You are too chicken-hearted to hear it." Juliet's chin rose up with indignation, but Sam pushed on. "You know, Scripture says perfect love casts out fear. Stop"—he enunciated the words slowly, carefully—"being afraid."

———

Slowly, Juliet walked down the hallway, reading the names on the doors. The gentleman downstairs told her that the Bureau of Military Information had not yet painted Robert's office door, as his promotion to major was still so new. Therefore, his was the only one without a name. Number 214. Third door down, on the right.

When she came to the door, she hugged the long, cylindrical, leather-wrapped package to her chest and knocked on the door.

"Come."

Robert's voice. Juliet's heart nearly beat out of her chest and she scolded herself for being ridiculous. What was the worst that could happen? She would humiliate herself and go home alone.

And she would crawl right back into her cave.

Lord, please let him...want me.

Slowly, she pushed the door open. Robert leaped to his feet at the sight of her. It had been years since she'd seen him in uniform and thought he was more handsome than ever in his blues. Clean-shaven, blond hair washed and curling up near his collar, she thought she could stare at him all day.

He flinched and pressed a hand to his chest. "Juliet. What a pleasant surprise."

"Still hurts, huh? It will, too. For a while."

"So the doctor informed me. But my breaths are good and deep. That's a good sign." He smiled warmly. "Why didn't you tell me you were coming?"

"Well, until I knocked on your door, I just wasn't sure if I had the courage to see you."

"I'm glad you did." He started to move, stopped, then came around the desk and hugged her. She nearly collapsed with joy when she laid her cheek on his chest. His arms set everything right in her world. "I have missed you more than I can say," he whispered. But a moment later, he released her. "But hugging a woman who is not my wife in my office is not conduct becoming of an officer."

"I notice your name isn't up there yet. Army in no hurry?"

His face fell a little. "I—I, um, am considering a transfer. Another month and this Credit Mobilier thing will be completely taken over by the Justice Department. I was thinking I'd like to go west, perhaps Colorado."

"It was beautiful." Unspoken words hung in there. She wanted to say she liked Colorado, too. Should she? Instead, she motioned with her odd-shaped package. "I brought you something."

She handed it to him. Puzzled, he surveyed it, rotating it in his hands. "What is it?"

"You have to open it." As he undid the leather ties, she told him, "I don't know how you'll feel about it. I kept my corset because I didn't want to forget the awful things I thought Hugh had done." The leather fell away and Robert stared at a white pine arrow, tipped with a fiercely sharp flint tip. "Now I keep the corset because it reminds me of all the good he did." She laid her hand over Robert's. "This is your arrow. The one you took trying to clear Hugh's name and bring a bad man to justice. I kept it, but after thinking about it, decided you should have it."

Robert looked over the arrow, from one end to the other, twice, while nodding. Finally, he said, "I can't accept this, Juliet." His refusal hit her like a good, swift kick from a mule. He handed it back to her. "I can't accept it...unless you'll make me a trade."

"A—a trade?"

"Yes. You see..." He turned, walked back to his desk, and lifted an open-topped box from the floor. Filled with various desk items, Juliet immediately saw the long, wooden shaft ending in feathers. Robert pulled the arrow from the box and walked back around to her. His lips twitched with a barely controlled smile. "I kept your arrow to remind *me* there was a reason you didn't die that day. God had saved you for something."

She didn't want to cry, but tears stung her eyes anyway. "Someone. He saved me for someone. If that someone wants me."

Robert took both the arrows, laid them on his desk, then slipped his arms around her. Juliet lost herself in those stunning blue eyes and guessed that therein lay a glimpse of heaven.

"What stories we have to tell our children." He kissed her and she savored—no, wallowed, rejoiced, *reveled*—in the feel of his arms around her, his lips on hers, the courage to open up her heart to him. "That is, Juliet," he whispered against her lips, "if you'll be my wife?"

Wife. Oh, yes. Yes.

Finally, unwavering, perfect love had cast out fear.

"Yes," she whispered. "Happily, joyfully, eternally yes."

Epilogue

Robert sat down on the settee. Had he ever been so tired? Had he ever been so glad anything like this was finished? Two years. Two years had flown by, ending in this defeat.

Overhead, the sounds of Juliet tucking little Courtney into bed—the soft, muffled voices of mother and daughter laughing and singing their funny little good night song—reminded him why he didn't *feel* defeated.

Smiling, he loosened his tie and settled back. Yes, he had lost the Senate race, and he had been confused at first by that, seeing as how he thought he had been called to run for Wilson's seat. But sitting here now, in the quiet—no crowds, no one slapping him on the back, no one wheeling-and-dealing with him—he could hear God more clearly.

Wilson's crimes had been exposed, Robert had been hailed as a hero, and the Washington machine had churned out a story of an up-and-coming star. A hero who would be a man of the people. At first, Robert's ego had been stroked enough to convince him he was on the right path. He'd pushed past the little, wiggling doubts squirming in the back of his mind.

Gradually, though, he'd become aware of the beguiling talk and obfuscated agendas swirling around him. People smiled at him, promised him things, but he'd begun to sense the lack of sincerity, could see the grins of wolves from the shadows. And as this train went faster and faster, Robert struggled to find time for God, and Juliet and Courtney.

His momentum with voters increasing, the election looked to be swinging in his favor. As it did, his dissatisfaction with this path grew exponentially. This very morning, he had cried out to God to make the way clear.

His loss had brought peace to his heart, and he had his answer.

Juliet swept down the stairs and into the drawing room, her blue silk-and-lace evening gown one of the most stunning things Robert had ever seen her wear. She was beautiful and still took his breath away, even after two years. He had so much for which to be thankful, how could he have let his friendship with God slip, even a little?

"Hmmm," she said, regarding him with a suspicious dip in her brow. "You don't look crushed."

"Should I be? Are you?" What if she was? His next step might be one that would make her unhappy. Perhaps she preferred Washington, had been looking forward to life as a senator's wife.

Juliet pulled two pins from her hair and let it fall like a golden waterfall cascading down her shoulders as she joined him on the settee. She leaned her head on his shoulder and sighed. "Would it crush you if I told you I didn't really want to be a senator's wife?"

Relief flooded his heart. He slipped his arm around her and rested his cheek on the top of her head. "I'm sorry. I got carried away. I thought I could make a difference, be an honest man in the Senate, but it all turned to..."

"Politics?"

He chuckled. "Yes. Politics. No selflessness. No honor. I'm glad I lost."

"Then I am too."

"I'm sorry for dragging you through it all."

"I didn't really mind. We were together. But, Robert..." She sat up and looked him squarely in the eye. "You do have a gift. You do care about people and the quality of their lives. Your quest was noble. I just don't think there is any honor in Washington."

"Do you think there is any honor anywhere?"

Her brow dipped as she pondered the question. "Some place that's still growing. Making its way. Building a future."

"Like Defiance?"

She gasped. "Believe it or not, that's exactly what I was thinking. I saw you talking to Charles McIntyre tonight."

"Yes, he said he came hoping a good man would win Wilson's seat, but if I lost, he had something to talk to me about. He wants to build Defiance into a town with a future. He wants honorable men in the city government." And this felt right. Hard work. Honest men. "I think God let me lose so I could see what was really important."

Juliet smiled, stroked his cheek. "Do you remember when you kissed me on the train the first time?"

"Remember? I waited ten years for that kiss, and afterward you looked like you wanted to jump over the rail."

"And now I don't want anything but to never leave you."

Every moment, Juliet made him grateful for love, hers and God's. How could he have ever been so caught up in politics to let his relationship with them both slip? He pulled her onto his lap and kissed her, longingly, deeply, till his head swam and she was glowing and breathless.

"Defiance or Timbuktu," she whispered, "Anywhere you go, I go."

"Then let's go to Defiance."

BONUS CONTENT
JULIET'S CORSET

Foreword

Juliet's Corset is a short story that fills in a missing span of years from my book, *Locket Full of Love*. The heroine, Juliet Watts, is just that: a heroine. A fire-breathing, strong-willed, pioneer woman...

Who actually lived.

She did survive an Indian attack, and her corset was—providentially—the reason.

Read on...

"I'm not afraid of storms, for I'm learning how to sail my ship."
—**Louisa May Alcott**

Chapter One

Juliet Watts stared at the tattered and bloody corset in her hands.

It gave the Indians some trouble, the young private had said. *It's cut up some, got a few punctures in it from knives, but when we pulled the arrow out of your chest, it was pretty clear the ribbing deflected the tip. The material slowed it down. That's what I call a miracle, Mrs. Watts.*

Juliet brushed her fingers over the little hole in the front. Crusted with blood, grimed over with dirt, and, yes, she could feel a nick in the steel boning. It probably had saved her life.

She should be amazed. Grateful. Glad to be breathing.

She was anything but.

Nightmares still plagued her, after four years. Hellish war cries filled her mind, hot, sweaty hands groped and tugged, determined fingers wound through her hair and snatched—it all still felt so real that goosebumps crawled her flesh.

The corset had been both a handle for the Indians to clutch and a stubborn obstacle to their desires. Consequently, they'd wasted precious time trying to work it off Juliet so they could have their way with her. But this lost time had allowed the Fourth Cavalry to make the outskirts of Rimfire. The

Comanche, therefore, had been forced to evacuate the town before burning it.

She lived. A town still stood.

All because of a corset?

Juliet shook her head. Sick of being preoccupied with the attack, she tossed the garment into her trunk and slammed the drawer. Part of her wanted to throw it away, part of her wanted to hang it up somewhere as a trophy. A trophy for what, though? Determination? Fortitude? Or just being lucky enough to survive a savage Indian attack?

Hugh had died in the attack—all because of some sudden and irrational desire to retrieve a cheap piece of jewelry.

Juliet felt abandoned and betrayed. By Hugh. By God. Even by the private who had come to see her in the hospital. He'd asked to pray for her and the request had struck Juliet as ridiculously insensitive and foolish. How dare he talk to her about a God who had saved her with a *corset* of all things—but her husband had been murdered right before her eyes?

The last thing she'd wanted was prayer. She'd wanted to be left alone. Pressured by friends in Texas, though, she'd moved to New York to be near family. And she'd been miserable in the city for the last four years.

Juliet glanced out the window at the moldy brick building across the alley, the sliver of gray sky above it. She still wanted to be alone, forgotten. Still wanted to go somewhere her name and her corset were as mundane as butter.

She was getting out of this city and had finally saved the money to do it.

Chapter Two

A wagon train from New York took Juliet to St. Joseph, Missouri. For no particular reason, when the train stopped here to restock, she decided to stay put. The town bustled and thrummed with activity, though its glory days of thousands and thousands of settlers heading west had slowed to a trickle.

Still, she liked the rhythm of the place and wandered down Sacramento Street. The wide Missouri and the bustling docks sat on her left. To her right, saloons, restaurants, hotels, and a few boarding houses gave the crews and passengers from the paddle wheelers warm beds and hot meals. A few blocks farther down, the businesses turned rowdier, or so she had heard. She had no interest there.

She scanned the busy street, freshly painted buildings and their false fronts gazing out on the rolling river. Juliet liked it here. St. Joe felt *homey*.

On a whim, she turned right at the next corner, onto Jackson Street. The main thoroughfare, which led traffic down to the riverfront, the traffic here on both the avenue and the boardwalk doubled. Several folks carrying valises and carpet-bags hurried down the hill to the docks behind her, probably trying to catch a steamer. Moving out of the center of the walk, closer to the businesses, she ambled along, glancing in the window of a bakery here, then a café there—

Juliet halted abruptly as a man slipped a For Sale sign in a window. Intrigued, she stepped back and scanned the entrance. A shingle hung over the door naming the place as the Lost Sally Saloon.

An idea teasing her brain, she pushed through the batwings and entered a narrow room. The bar stretched across the back. Two windows down each side of the building lent more light and lightheartedness than was normal for this type of establishment. Several of the tables were occupied by men enjoying a sandwich and beer for lunch.

Juliet did not get the impression that the Lost Sally was a wild saloon, though, for this time of day, she supposed it was hard to tell. The patrons paid her only fleeting glances as she walked back to the bar. The man who had put the sign in the window, a middle-aged, heavy-set man with a grizzled face, had his back to her.

"Excuse me."

He spun, a bottle of whiskey topped with a funnel in his hand. "Yes, ma'am. What can I do for ya?"

"Are you the owner?"

"No, ma'am. But I am the manager." He set the bottle down and smiled, the friendliness of the expression reaching his dark eyes and softening his bulldog face. "I can probably help you."

"Is this place profitable?"

"It don't lose money. Some months is better than others, but it's steady."

"Why is the owner selling?"

"Don't know. Didn't ask. Just hoping the new owner keeps me on."

"What's he selling? The business and the inventory or just the building?"

"Far as I know, he's selling the whole shooting match."

Juliet turned and glanced around the saloon. "What's the owner's name?"

"Winnert Tailor."

"Could you please see if you could get Mr. Tailor to meet me here later today?"

"You interested in buying the Lost Sally?"

She came back to him, smiling. "I believe so, unless the price is outlandish."

Chapter Three

When Juliet returned to the Lost Sally at 3:00, one Mr. Percival Frink was there to meet her. A man wearing an expensive, tailored suit and sternly slick-backed hair, she guessed he wasn't the owner either.

"I am not," he told her. "I represent the owner," Frink said, jutting out his hand. "I am his attorney, and he asked me to handle the sale of his saloon."

"Why is he selling?" she asked, accepting the handshake.

"He bought the Lost Sally at a public auction. On a whim, you could say. He discovered he does not care for the saloon business. He wants to explore other entrepreneurial avenues."

Juliet drifted her fingers down the bar as she walked behind it. Trying on the feel of the place, she laid both hands on the polished wood and surveyed the room, the few patrons quietly enjoying their ale. "I was told the saloon makes money, even if not a lot. I'd be able to look at the books, of course?"

"Of course. And, yes, the Lost Sally turns a steady profit, though not a huge one. But that is with no promotion by the current owner. An enterprising owner could do more, I'm quite sure."

Would Juliet be an enterprising owner? She thought she could be. She dragged her hands back and squared her shoulders. "Let's talk dollars."

Chapter Four

Juliet was delighted to learn the Lost Sally had a small apartment upstairs. She had bought a business and a home in one fell swoop. It needed a good dusting and linens for the bed, but the simple room with its pot-bellied stove would do.

She pulled open the drawer on her trunk and sighed at the sight of her corset. Why did she keep that thing around? She picked it up, contemplating tossing it in the stove and burning it.

"My, that looks like it's got a story behind it." Sam, the grizzled, weathered bartender she'd met the day she found the saloon, stood in the doorway, her easel and art supplies in his hand.

Juliet sucked on her cheek, the memories flashing through her mind as fast as lightning. "Saved the woman's life who was wearing it."

"No kidding?" Sam stepped in and set the art supplies on the bed, his pockmarked, gritty face alight with curiosity. He peered around Juliet for a better look. Not nearly as enamored with it as he appeared to be, she handed it to him.

The big man inspected the undergarment carefully, pausing over every tear, every rip, and especially the rust colored hole in the front. "Saved her life, eh?" After a moment, his hand stilled. "I remember hearing tell years ago of a woman the Comanches tried to...*harm* and the corset stopped an arrow." He regarded Juliet with one raised brow and narrowed eyes. "I thought that was just another tall tale out of Texas. How'd you come by this?"

She almost offered a dismissive answer but gave in to his curiosity out of sheer weariness. "It was me," she said flatly. "I was wearing that corset when the Comanche hit Rimfire. I survived. My husband did not."

Sam's expression melted into sympathy and he nodded. "I'm sorry for your loss."

She plucked the corset from his hands and tossed it back into her trunk. "Yes. Thank you."

With her back to Sam, she thought he might understand she was done discussing the past, but he didn't leave. A moment later, he moved off to her left so he could see her profile. "Ain't really any of my business, but the busiest saloon in town has a twelve-foot stuffed grizzly on display. The owner shot it up in Montana territory. It brings in a lot of people to the Big Bear Saloon."

Was he suggesting...? Juliet cut her eyes at him. "You think I should...?" What *was* he saying?

"I think a lot more men in this town would rather see the Iron Rose of Texas and the garment that saved her life."

"The Iron—" *The Iron Rose?* She'd never heard the name. It both horrified her and flattered her. After a moment's thought, however, she decided she did not wish to perpetuate what it implied. "I don't think I want that moniker." She sat down on the bed. "I'm alive because I wore a corset they had no idea how to undo. I didn't fight them off single-handedly in wild combat." She swallowed against the knot forming in her throat. "I'm no Calamity Jane. I just got lucky."

Sam scratched his chin thoughtfully, then shoved his hands

into his pockets and nodded. "Seems to me, God was watching out for you."

She clamped her jaws. She hated hearing that. People who said that didn't wake up in the middle of the night, bathed in sweat, choking back a scream caused by nightmares so real...

She sighed and stood up again, ready to end this conversation. "Thank you, Sam," she said curtly. "I'll see you downstairs in a bit."

His face, wise, wrinkled, melted a little in obvious hurt, and Juliet felt as if she'd kicked a dog. But she couldn't talk about God...He was too cruel, too distant. If He was really a loving God, maybe one day He'd shove past her anger and show Himself, but she wasn't holding her breath.

Chapter Five

Juliet had worked with Hugh enough in their mercantile to understand the inventory management of a saloon. Not to mention, Sam was a great help. No, the hard part about running a saloon was managing the patrons. Bossy, arrogant, sometimes inebriated, expecting things from Juliet they had no business expecting.

Tired of the perpetual battle to protect her reputation, she pushed a beer across the bar and frowned at the grinning, hopeful sailor reaching for it. "I said no, James, and my *no* means exactly that."

In his late twenties perhaps, tanned and lined from life in the elements, he was man enough to understand her meaning. Yet, a devilish glee still played around his lips and she was wary. He was a River Rat, as these men called themselves. They ran the Missouri and the Mississippi aboard paddle wheelers and flatboats, only stepping ashore long enough to entertain themselves for an evening and then back to the water they went. They didn't seem to have many rules and even fewer boundaries.

Well, Juliet was not here for his or any other Rat's entertainment. "For the hundredth time," she said slowly, "you can get beer or liquor here and that is all."

James huffed and drummed his fingers on the mug of beer. The men on each side of him chuckled knowingly. Juliet had given them the same speech.

"Beer and liquor," he repeated, his heavy Southern drawl drenching his words.

She gave him a slow, acquiescent dip of her chin.

"But see," he leaned forward and lowered his voice, "you're so pretty. I was thinking about you out on the wide water yesterday. I've got a silver eagle burning a hole in my pocket, just for you—"

"James," Juliet snapped, losing her patience. "There are plenty of pretty girls down at the other end of the street." Her raised voice drew the attention of several nearby patrons. A few smiled. A few did not. Hungry stares argued a consensus was growing that Juliet should add herself to the list of drafts available in the Lost Sally. She moistened her lips and took a moment to calm down. "I think that beer is your last one here tonight."

Out of the corner of her eyes, Juliet saw Sam, wiping the bar, slow his pace. He was listening, she knew. Wondering if he'd need to escort the man out. So far, Sam had not been called upon to do so, the evicted customers had moved on voluntarily. Something in James's expression changed, however, turned unfriendly, and she recognized the look of a man who did not like to retreat.

"You puzzle me, Miss Juliet."

A hand snaked out between James and the man beside him and slapped two bits down on the bar. Juliet swiped up the coin and reached for a clean mug. "Why do I puzzle you, James?" she asked blandly, pouring a beer for the waiting customer. Pasting on a tense smile, she slid the drink across the bar to him, but didn't see him. Just another faceless patron.

"I own my own vessel," James said, an edge in his voice. "I

have a fine cabin just off the pilot house. We could have a nice, quiet evening together, you and me."

Juliet snapped her gaze back to him, done caring if she made a scene. Absently, she noted Sam whispering to patrons down the bar. "James, why must you make me be rude?" Their eyes locked and she hoped the sailor would drop this pursuit. "You're not hearing me."

His lip curled. "I'm no regular River Rat." Jaws clenched, he pushed his untouched beer away. "I've got plans and a future." His voice began to rise. "I'll own my own shipping company in a few years. I'll be somebody important."

Juliet wondered what James was trying to express. Why did it seem so important to him to have her respect? Or perhaps he just wanted respect in general. "Good. Fine. Wonderful. You'll be able to afford all the trollops you can handle." She spoke the next words with careful enunciation. "But I won't be one of them."

Again, she noted Sam whispering to customers at the bar, and out at the tables, others were whispering as well, as if some news or story was spreading. James was oblivious. His face flushed now with anger, he stepped back from his drink and waved an accusing finger at Juliet. "You aren't any better than any other woman in this town."

"I never said I was. And since I've owned the Lost Sally, I haven't had to throw anyone out, but if you don't calm down, you'll be the first."

"All you Yankees are the same," he spat. "Thinking you're so much better, tougher, smarter than the rest of the world."

Juliet was done. "Get out. You're banned from the Lost Sally. Don't come back."

"Don't come back." He shook his head. "I oughta carry you outta here over my shoulder. Show you what a Mississippi man can do with a woman—"

"Son." An older gentleman with a head full of thick, white hair appeared from behind him. He laid a light hand on James's shoulder and squeezed. "The lady's right. You should find entertainment elsewhere."

James swept off the fingers and rounded on the intruder. "This is none of your affair, old man."

"Back in '67, I lost a son in the Texas Indian Wars. This here lady survived one of the raids. You show her some respect."

Juliet cut her eyes at Sam. He'd told.

James deflated a little, wavered with uncertainty, then turned back to Juliet. "Is that true?"

The room fell completely silent. Sam urged her with a subtle nod to confess. Juliet ran her tongue over her teeth, pondering James's question. "Yes." An audible gasp escaped from the room of rough and rowdy men. "Rimfire. The Comanche killed my husband." She added no other details.

James sucked in his bottom lip and stared at the ground.

The old man who had interrupted James surveyed Juliet with a pained expression. "You wouldn't happen to be the Iron Rose, would you, ma'am?"

Before she could decide how to answer, a man stepped out from the shadows up near the front door. "There's no way," he yelled across the room. "The papers made all that up."

Juliet swallowed. She understood what Sam had tried to do. Establish her. Protect her. Create a mystique that would ensure her safety. Would it work? Twenty or more pairs of eyes waited for the answer, rapt with anticipation. "I still have the corset."

Again, the room gasped together as if all these men were one astonished creature.

Juliet took a deep breath, splayed her hands out on the bar to hold herself up. "Come back tomorrow and you'll see it."

Chapter Six

Well, there it is.

Sighing, Juliet stepped back from the ragged corset laced over the dress form standing at the end of the bar. Her gaze drifted over the filthy undergarment pockmarked with holes and smeared with crimson handprints. Each streak, each drop of blood, each fraying tear in the cloth made her heart race.

And now here it was for the world to ogle.

She pinched sweat off her upper lip and rotated her shoulders, trying to lose the tension. Yes, it was all still clear in her head...except why she was doing this. Why put the horrid thing on display?

Why had she kept it? What did it mean to her? What had compelled her to drag it from Texas to New York to Missouri?

She tilted her head, pondering. Was the corset a bitter memorial to her foolish husband? Or to her inability to forgive him for his foolishness? Sam seemed to think she kept the corset because it was a testimony to the protection the Almighty had wielded over her that day.

Juliet didn't buy that. The Lord above couldn't care less about her. If He cared at all, Hugh wouldn't be dead. She wouldn't be alone. She wouldn't be bitter.

"You ever talk about it?"

Sam's voice didn't startle her. She found his presence and his tone comforting. She did not respond, however, only kept her gaze on the corset as he walked around behind the bar.

"To anybody?"

Juliet folded her arms and shrugged against a sudden chill. "No." *I prefer to carry all the memories around in my brain, letting them squirm and fight like snakes.* "I don't need to. I'm fine." She'd said that a million times over the, what, last seven years? Why did it feel like a lie when she said it to Sam?

Because they both knew it was.

Chapter Seven

As customers drifted in that afternoon and evening, Juliet was amazed at their reactions. Staring at the corset and then the woman who had survived the attack instantly brought about a change in her patrons.

At first, she couldn't put her finger on it. The conversations were less boisterous, the glances her way more polite, appreciative. The thinly veiled arrogance men normally had for a working woman had been tamped down out of sight. They said *please* and *thank you* to her when ordering their drinks and food. Even strangers who had never stepped into the Lost Sally before almost seemed in awe of Juliet after gaping at the corset for a moment.

It dawned on her that this was what true respect looked like.

Sam had been right.

Marveling over the changes, she slipped out of the room to retrieve a fresh case of liquor from storage. When she reemerged, she noted the din of the saloon's noises had softened even more, to a somber rumble like dying thunder. Sam nodded to his left and stepped back to clear the view.

James was standing before the mannequin, staring transfixed at the corset. Juliet set the box of whiskey on the bar and waited. Somehow, she knew this was a watershed moment. If the garment, the story behind it—if Juliet—didn't impress a River Rat, she'd be fighting men off till she was old and gray.

As if feeling her stare, James slowly slid his gaze down the bar to her. "I owe you an apology. And I'll see to it that everyone on both the Mississippi and the Missouri knows about the Iron Rose."

The room fell graveyard silent. All eyes turned to Juliet. She could almost feel their stares clawing at her, waiting for a response. That confounded garment had labeled her the Iron Rose—a woman of fortitude and virtue. A woman to be respected. She could pick up the moniker and run with it, protect her saloon, live a peaceable life...

Or tell them all she hated the thing and the foolhardy husband it represented.

Worn down, she was ready for life to be a little easier, even if she had yet to make peace with Hugh and his choice. She raised her chin.

In time, she told herself, in time, the legend would die. This, tonight, was a start. "Well, if you were to do that, James..." Juliet picked up a customer's shot of whiskey and held it high for a toast. "You would be welcome in the Lost Sally." She raised the glass even higher and turned to her customers. "This round is on the Iron Rose, gentlemen!"

The room erupted in cheers and Sam smiled knowingly at Juliet. Well, he'd proven his point. This ridiculous garment had saved her life, and now it seemed it would not only save her reputation but guarantee her a prosperous business as well.

Juliet hadn't made peace with it—not the garment, not the events, not even God—but for the time being, she'd play the hand she'd been dealt. Grudgingly, she dipped her head and smiled wryly at her bartender.

Touché, Sam. Touché.

A Look At: Carolina Homecoming

Even in the shadows of the Blue Ridge, war will find them.

Widowed by the Civil War, Ruth Grant joins her grieving mother-in-law on a journey back to the foothills of the Blue Ridge Mountains, seeking refuge in a land untouched by the conflict that shattered their lives. But peace proves elusive, even in the quiet hills of Upstate South Carolina.

Noemie returns home to reclaim her family farm, only to find a greedy cousin trying to steal it from under her. As tensions rise, the women find an unexpected ally in Montgomery Boaze—the region's wealthiest landowner, a steady presence with a guarded heart and a past full of pain.

Montgomery has no intention of letting his kin be cheated. But protecting Noemie—and the strong, spirited Ruth—pulls him into a deeper struggle, one that stirs long-buried feelings and challenges everything he believes about loyalty, justice, and love.

As land disputes turn dangerous and old wounds resurface, Ruth and Montgomery must decide: can broken hearts learn to trust again? And in a world still reeling from war, is love worth the risk?

A tale of second chances, quiet faith, and the battles worth fighting—where the true war is not North versus South, but heart versus heart.

AVAILABLE OCTOBER 2025

About the Author

Heather Blanton is a *USA Today* bestselling author of thirty Christian Western romances, including the highly rated and awarded Romance in the Rockies series. She is also an award-winning script writer. Her Romance in the Rockies series has been optioned for a limited TV series, and her script *Unbridled Hearts* is currently optioned as well.

She grew up in the mountains of Western North Carolina on a steady diet of *Bonanza, Gunsmoke,* and John Wayne Westerns. Her daddy taught her to shoot when she was five, and she can hit that at which she aims.

Her novels are all Christian Western romance because she enjoys creating feisty pioneer women who struggle to find love and hold on to their faith. Like all good, old-fashioned Westerns, there is always justice, a moral message, American values, lots of high adventure, unexpected plot twists, and often a touch of suspense.

www.authorheatherblanton.com